Tc

Uniform Encounters
Set Ablaze
Arresting Behaviour
Lust Emergency
Guarded Desires
Secret Fire
Dangerous Wish

Gin & Jazz
Hollywood Bound
Razzle Dazzle
Tarnished Glitter
Starring Role
Studio Orders
Casting Call
Play Acting

Sin City Uniforms
All Fired Up

Clandestine Classics
The Legend of Sleepy Hollow
The Fall of the House of Usher

What's his Passion?
Rockin' the Alternative

Sin City Uniforms

ALL FIRED UP

To Lou –
It's been great to spend
some time getting to know
you! Hugs –
Morticia Knight

MORTICIA KNIGHT

All Fired Up
ISBN # 978-1-78430-240-5

Interior text design by Claire Siemaszkiewicz
Totally Bound Publishing

Published in 2014 by Totally Bound Publishing, Newland House, The Point, Weaver Road, Lincoln, LN6 3QN, United Kingdom.

Totally Bound Publishing is an imprint of Total-E-Ntwined Limited.

ALL FIRED UP

Dedication

A hearty thanks to Crystal Marie for allowing me to purloin one of her trademarked expressions. Yuppers, she is one fine minx.

Chapter One

Thorin Oakenshield and Michael Jackson strolled together down the Strip, hips bumping, singing *Beat It* rather loudly—and badly. There was a valiant attempt on their part to keep their tall, pink, plastic cocktail glasses from sloshing their drinks everywhere by holding them up as they swung their arms and asses around. They were having limited success. As they continued with their boisterous dancing, the two men knocked into a young woman, almost toppling her off her glittery platform stilettos.

Officer Shawn Everly picked up his pace, jogging to catch up to them. He couldn't deny that being assigned to foot patrol along Las Vegas Boulevard was anything but dull. After reaching the two happy carousers, he tapped Thorin on the shoulder. Whirling around, the Dwarven leader almost dumped his cocktail on Shawn.

"Oh, hey… Sorry, Officer. I…uh…"

Shawn resisted the urge to break out laughing at the mortified expression on the partier's face.

"We have an unusually crowded night out here, gentlemen. There are families with young kids and we don't anyone to get hurt—yourselves included."

Michael Jackson piped in, swaying on his feet a bit. "He's cool. Fought a dragon and shit. He's even got a sword for protection."

He indicated to the fake weapon attached to his friend's costume belt. Obviously Michael was less in control of his senses than his fellow reveler. Shawn turned back to Thorin.

"Are we gonna have any problems with you two out here tonight?"

He shook his head vigorously. "No sir, we're just having fun like everyone else, but we'll be more careful."

Shawn gave him a curt nod, desperately trying to maintain his composure. "Good. I don't want to hear any complaints about either one of you, okay?"

"You've got it, Officer."

"Oh, and Thorin?"

"Yes, sir?"

"Good luck with Smaug."

The man stared at Shawn as if he'd lost his mind. It took a moment, but he finally snorted laughter.

"Yeah, thanks, Officer."

The two men carried on, picking up where they'd left off—but reining it in a bit. Shawn glanced around at the barely controlled chaos. Colorful neon and flashing lights were enough to keep him on sensory overload, but it was also combined with honking horns, wildly dressed people, yelling, laughter, and music, all set against the backdrop of spectacularly grand resort casinos.

His radio crackled to life. He'd moved far enough down the Boulevard that he'd gotten separated from his partner amongst the crush of humanity filling the sidewalk.

"Where is your position, Vicki?"

"I'm at the Bellagio. We've got a drunk swimming around in the lake in front of the shops."

"Is he responding to your orders to get out?"

"Nope."

Shawn pressed his lips together. The damn lake was a constant issue—it was way too tempting in the scorching desert heat. Even though it was almost seven o'clock at night, it was still over a hundred degrees. At least August was almost over. He'd been assured by the other officers that it would eventually become bearable. Since he'd only recently arrived in Vegas at the end of May, all he'd encountered so far was *un*bearable.

"On my way."

As he wove in and out of the crowds, he spotted a cruiser pulled over. There was an officer talking to a group of sparkling and scantily clad women. He recognized Sergeant Darren Miller of the Homeland Security Saturation Team. Like Shawn, he was assigned to the Convention Center Area Command that comprised the majority of the world-famous Las Vegas Strip. When Shawn got closer, he picked up the tail end of the conversation.

"...over the highway. It's a five minute walk from here to the Mirage and you can take the bridge walkway there to get to the other side. Stay out of the street, ladies, it's very dangerous. We want you to have a good time here—not get hurt."

One of the women moved closer to him, as if she was about to give him a hug. He stepped back and placed his hands in front of him in a blocking gesture.

"Step back, please."

"But I wanted to thank you. You're so sexy. I love your uniform."

Shawn smirked. Law enforcement in Las Vegas was definitely unique. It had been quite the culture shock from his previous experiences as part of the Gang Task Force in Los Angeles.

His fellow Metropolitan Police Department officer finally succeeded in getting the women to move along and turned his attention to Shawn. A casual observer would no doubt wonder if they worked for the same agency. Shawn wore a bright yellow uniform shirt that helped him to stand out amidst the overwhelming amount of people walking around. The MPD officers in cruisers wore khaki uniforms and so did the mounted patrol.

"Hey, Darren, we've got a drunk in the lake."

Darren rolled his eyes. "Is he reachable or are they gonna have to use one of the boats?"

"Not sure. I'm headed over there now."

"Radio it in. It's so out of control tonight, Parker and I need to stay on the street."

As if in confirmation, a white stretch limo crawled by in the gridlocked traffic. A woman stood with the top half of her body peeking out of the sunroof. She was yelling and flashing her breasts to the cheering sidewalk crowds.

Darren lowered his head and shook it, seemingly in resignation. He lifted it quickly and shouted out to his partner.

"Let's go, Parker!"

It wouldn't exactly be a high speed chase, considering how squashed together foot and vehicle traffic was. At least with the cruiser's lights flashing, there was the opportunity to clear a path to get to the limo. The weekends were killers. No room to breathe.

Bathroom and food breaks next to impossible. But he currently had an inebriated bather to deal with. Before he took off in the direction of the luxurious resort again, he contacted dispatch to apprise them of the situation and to request backup.

He jogged over to the hotel at a fast clip. As soon as he spied his partner, Vicki Ruiz, he wound his way through the people seemingly lost in their own revelry. No doubt they were also overwhelmed by the magical and decadent surroundings. And liquor. He had to speak up to be heard, and to get the circle of onlookers surrounding his partner to step aside. At last he reached her and saw what they were up against.

The man splashing around in the lake laughed and shouted obscenities at the crowd. Then he would dive under the water when someone lobbed a plastic cup or other random object as they yelled back at him. Occasionally he would throw handfuls of change at his hecklers—riches he had no doubt scooped up from the bottom of the cement lake. It was too much for the two of them to keep under control by themselves.

Despite how unruly everything was, Vicki appeared completely unfazed. Since she had a good five years on him in terms of dealing with Vegas tourists, there was very little that ever flustered her.

"There you are, Everly. Thought I was stuck with drunken boy on my own."

"I thought about joining him. It's a bitch of a hot night."

"Yeah. No kidding. I contacted hotel management to get one of their guys out here to man one of the rescue boats."

She paused to yell at a man and woman grinding and groping each other. The carouser had a one liter bottle of some sort of alcohol dangling precariously out of his back pocket.

"Hey, you two! Save it for the clubs! And I don't want to see that bottle break on my sidewalk. Take it out of your pants *now*."

The couple complied, meaning that he and Vicki wouldn't have to add dealing with them to their current list of things to do.

"They know to cancel the dancing waters show?"

"Yuppers."

The spectacular fountain show—complete with five-hundred-foot-high-choreographed jet streams of water and a mixture of classical and pop music—would be a disaster to someone paddling around in the water.

"Good. I called this in, so we should have some additional units out here soon."

"Let's hope." She had the beginnings of a furrow on her brow. "It's getting rowdier by the second."

She was right. The man in the water was becoming more and more hostile toward the crowd and they were reciprocating with equal vitriol. Once the Bellagio's crew got out there, they would have to also add to their agenda the retrieval of more than the usual bits of floating trash out of the lake.

Two guys began pushing one another next to the mid-torso high stone balustrade that edged the water. Shawn lunged toward them.

"Knock it off!" He wedged himself in between the much taller men and pushed them apart. He made up for his height with his strength. "Do you really want to have your fun night in Vegas end in jail?"

"He started it!"

Shawn glared up at the indignant troublemaker. "Not interested. I'm only interested in both of you stopping. *Immediately*. Got it?"

The other man held up his hands in acquiescence. "Got it. My brother and I won't be any more of a problem."

Brother? Nice.

"Good. Now get out of here."

The troublemaker spoke up again. "But we're only watching that guy like everyone else—"

"*What* did I just say?"

"Come on, Larry."

The reasonable brother yanked on his sibling's arm and they moved away, but not without some barely concealed angry mutterings. There were a few generic law enforcement slurs that were audible, but Shawn found them laughable. If the surly brother wanted to learn some real insults, he needed to hang out in LA for a while. That was the one good thing Shawn had taken away from his previous assignment—an extraordinarily tough skin.

He turned back to Vicki and saw that her worry lines had increased. On her, it practically amounted to hysteria. He relied on Vicki's judgment quite a bit. She was much more attuned to the beat of the Strip. If she was concerned, then things had to be deteriorating. Since the last fountain show was getting canceled because of the drunk in the lake, the large unruly crowd would no doubt be very unhappy. After pulling out his cell, he speed-dialed the Bellagio's management. All of the major resorts' numbers were programmed into his department-issued phone.

"This is Officer Everly on scene with the incident at the lake. I need someone for that boat out here right away. And can you bring up any more lights? "

The resort assured him that it was going as fast as it could, but that it couldn't add any more lights. He eyed the drunken tourist swimming and splashing around. So far, the man seemed okay, but beyond any other considerations was the fact that his inebriated state combined with being in the water was extremely dangerous. It would be too easy for him to accidentally take in too much water and drown—particularly with all the diving under the surface he'd been doing.

It had taken Shawn at least the first week after he'd been on duty to get accustomed to the idea that people could drink openly on the streets of Vegas. That was definitely not the case back in LA or other places in general. For the most part, everyone was in Sin City to have fun—they had no interest in causing trouble. But with over a hundred thousand people converging on the small concentrated strip area on a daily basis—even more on the weekends—there was bound to be trouble. Sometimes it was nothing more than drunkenness gone wrong—other times it would be a brutal murder. It was a round the clock, non-stop party town. They were constantly on alert.

When Vicki's previous partner had relocated a couple of months back, Shawn had grabbed the opportunity. He'd had enough of fighting the continuous threat of violent gangs in Los Angeles. Once he'd officially been offered the position from the LVMPD, he'd moved himself to Vegas. Hard work and danger didn't bother him. The sense of accomplishment he had as a task force team member, taking gang members off the street, had kept him working in that division for several years. But it had exacted a toll.

He'd been a police officer for over a decade and he'd passed thirty a few years back. He hadn't been able to maintain a steady relationship in what had amounted to forever—not when any of the men he'd ever gotten involved with had found it impossible to handle the crazy hours and the unusual risks Shawn took on a daily basis. Starting over somewhere completely different had seemed like an excellent idea. Getting away from his homophobe brother had been even better. The rest of his family tolerated him, but not enough to motivate him to stay in Los Angeles forever.

"Oh shit! He hasn't come back up yet!"

One of the onlookers pointed in the direction of where the swimmer had been only seconds before. All that remained were small ripples on the surface of the water.

Goddammit.

Moving quickly, Shawn tore off his duty belt, frantically toeing off his shoes as he did. Before Vicki had the opportunity to register what was happening, Shawn thrust the equipment at her. To her credit, she wordlessly grabbed it. He boosted himself over the banister and dropped into the water—it wasn't deep enough at the banks for him to dive safely, only about four feet. But it was fucking *cold,* much more so than he'd expected. Shawn gritted his teeth and swam desperately toward the dark shape floating just below the surface of the lake. He was soaking wet but his mouth was dry. His heart beat wildly as he propelled himself forward.

By the time he reached the victim, he was no longer able to touch the bottom at all. He turned the man over, wrapping his arm around his chest, keeping his head above water. Shawn's muscles burned with the stress of hauling the limp weight of the unconscious drunk to safety through the frigid waters, and from swimming using only one arm to pull them both along.

Taking in big gulps of air, he noted that several emergency vehicles had arrived. He could barely make out the yellow engine that he was certain would be from nearby Station 32. There were additional police units, the red truck of Las Vegas Fire and Rescue, as well as at least one ambulance.

The drunk awoke with a start, choking and gasping, fighting Shawn's attempts to save his life. Shawn was pulled under. He'd barely had a chance to take a breath. His feet hit the bottom and Shawn propelled both of them back up out of the water. It was only a few seconds before he was dragged under again. Weakening, Shawn tried once more, but he barely broke the surface. Right as he sucked in a breath, he was yanked down and he took in more water than air.

Oh shit. Might be drowning.

His lungs burned. He sputtered under the surface and fought not to inhale again, but it was impossible. His body's natural instinct to draw in air took over and he sucked in more cold water. He was disoriented and dizzy, not sure how much longer he could last.

Keep fighting, keep kicking! Right as he was at the edge of unconsciousness, strong arms encircled his waist and lifted him well above the water line. He knew not to fight, to allow himself to be guided, but he couldn't stop himself from coughing violently, his body doing everything it could to expel the unwanted liquid from his airways.

"I've got you. Hang tight. We're almost there."

No way. Trent Marshall.

He would've recognized the deep growl of Station 32 firefighter Trent anywhere. As much as he wanted to be thrilled that he was finally being held by his first local crush, he was more concerned with staying alive. He still gasped and choked, but other than the strong ache in his lungs and the fact that he was inexplicably freezing, he was sure he'd be okay.

Trent saved me.

The world was a crazy place and Vegas was the craziest. He'd only met the guy one time at a Clark County blood drive organized by the police and fire agencies and he'd been certain that their attraction was mutual. When Trent had shaken his hand politely and walked away, Shawn figured he must have read too much into the way Trent had looked him over throughout that afternoon. And here he was being held by the man.

They reached the banks of the lake and Shawn was finally able to put his feet down. Wanting to maintain a small portion of his dignity, he loosened what he realized had been a death grip on Trent and attempted to stand on his own. His legs immediately gave out and he would've fallen face first back into the water if Trent hadn't caught him.

"Let me help you, Shawn."

He remembers my name?

Trent wrapped his arms around Shawn's torso and guided him to the edge of the water. The crowds cheered and he noted that two other firefighters leaned over the balustrade, ready to haul him up and over. He was frustrated as hell that his normally strong limbs wouldn't allow him to do it himself, his muscles still like jelly.

Moving behind him, Trent then grasped his waist with his large hands and lifted him up right as the other men grabbed his arms. Just as he was being pulled up by the rescuers, Trent planted one of his strong hands on Shawn's ass and gave him a hearty push. He cleared the top of the stone barrier, groaning over the fact that he'd been publically felt up by a sexy firefighter.

He supposed that was an exaggeration, but he couldn't help but be a tad embarrassed. First he'd had to be saved—then everyone had seen him get groped by Trent.

The extra officers who had shown up for support held the crowds back as a stretcher was brought through. The sight of it jarred something in him.

"Where's the guy who was in the lake?"

"You mean the dumbass?"

Shawn peered up at Trent. He wanted to say something, but instead all he managed was a lame nod. As he'd almost just drowned, he hoped Trent would excuse him for not being more articulate. The gurney stopped next to Shawn and Trent pushed on his shoulder, encouraging him to sit. One paramedic wrapped a blanket around his shoulders while another took his vitals. Still Trent stood there, towering over him—looking at him.

Holy Christ. Say something already.

Trent crossed his arms over his body, almost defiantly. "Don't worry about that guy. He's been transported already."

Trent continued to stare. Shawn wriggled. His soggy briefs were scrunched in his crack and his balls were being uncomfortably smashed. Not a good combination.

"You must be pretty strong. I bet that drunk has a hundred pounds on you."

Shawn couldn't tell if he was being complimented or mocked. That was the one thing he'd noticed when he'd spoken with Trent that day at the blood drive—the monotone sound of his voice. Not that the deep timbre wasn't as sexy as hell—it was—but it was difficult to read. It sort of reminded him of Clint Eastwood—or John Wayne. Somewhere in between. He must have had a questioning expression on his face.

"Are you all right?"

"Huh? Oh, yeah. Sorry, still trying to process all of this."

One of the medics interrupted. "Officer Everly, can you tell me where you are and what just happened?"

He couldn't help but frown, even though he knew the EMT was simply doing his job.

"Yes. I'm in front of the Bellagio and I tried to retrieve a misbehaving tourist from the drink."

Trent made a sound that came out as a combination of a grunt and a snort. "That's a charitable way to put it."

Shawn chuckled and gazed up at Trent, noting the steel blue eyes that had captured him when he first met the firefighter. Since Shawn was only about five foot nine and Trent was at least six foot two, the sensation that he loomed over him was even sharper with him seated and Trent standing. A slight smirk tugged at the corners of Trent's mouth. Shawn figured the guy was likely mid-thirties, but he had what appeared to be a permanently established deep tan. His hair was a sandy sun-bleached blond that had probably leaned more toward brown at one time. Lines in his forehead and around his eyes were noticeable, but did nothing to detract from his masculine good looks. Shawn couldn't even begin to contemplate Trent's well-built body. It wouldn't help him feel any better about himself to get hard in front of not only his associates, but also the tourists as well. He'd been treated to the sight of Trent's muscular physique at the blood drive when all that the firefighter had worn was a form fitting T-shirt and shorts.

Another medic came over and handed Trent a blanket and started to try to take his vitals too. He accepted the blanket but shot the EMT a glare that could've given children nightmares, and the poor guy backed off. Shawn was reminded that Trent had also braved the bizarrely freezing waters of the Bellagio fountain.

"Sorry you had to come after me like that."

It wasn't the most eloquent thing to say, but he *had* just gone through a near-death experience. He assured himself that he shouldn't be expected to come up with anything too amazing.

"Don't be ridiculous. The only person who should be sorry is the—"

"Dumbass?"

Trent made the smirking face again, narrowing his eyes as he nodded at Shawn.

Which means…?

The spark was back. A dose of attraction. But would they do anything about it this time?

Right then, a news van pulled up. It parked next to one that he hadn't noticed was already there. Since parking was never allowed right on the Strip, it was a good bet that that side of the Boulevard had been closed off as soon as the emergency vehicles had arrived. He spotted Vicki and Darren keeping the reporters back.

When he turned to finally say something to Trent, he was surprised to see he'd walked away. He didn't want to appear too obvious by searching him out, so he subtly glanced around. First he brought the blanket up over his head—not a bad idea anyway with the press trying to get photos—and used it to shield himself.

After catching a glimpse of Trent over by the engine talking to the driver, he realized he was being goofy. He'd almost drowned in a fucking phony lake at a casino and he was trying to hook up with the fireman who'd rescued his sorry ass.

Beyond pathetic.

Sure, he was lonely—the new guy in town and all that—but he didn't need to take it to extremes, even though he *had* already been interested in fireman Marshall from the first moment he'd spied the brawny looker. Still, trying to get a date under the current circumstances was probably not the brainiest of ideas he'd ever had. He could wait. There was a definite attraction. He had no clue as to why Trent had walked away after they'd first met or why he'd done it again, but that wouldn't stop him.

Never shoulda looked at me like that if you didn't want to play.

Chapter Two

Trent made sure to keep his body angled in a way so that he could keep an eye on Officer Shawn Everly. He didn't want the cop to catch him gazing in his direction, but he couldn't stop himself from doing that very thing.

So cute. Dammit.

Their first handshake at the blood drive had almost done him in. There had been an instant zing when their skin had touched. Everything about the officer who had been dressed in a muscle baring T-shirt had appealed to him.

He was sure Shawn was at least thirty—based on his years in the force—however, he appeared younger. Shawn had wavy brown hair that was trimmed in a stylishly short cut. He'd been fascinated by the cop's intense hazel eyes with gold flecks in them that had seemed to change color as he spoke. His features were angular, his mouth wide and perfect when he smiled. Even though Shawn was shorter, he had a confident and strong presence. Trent had noted that he was very friendly, unassuming—that had been a huge turn on.

It was also obvious that Shawn was a man who took care of himself. It had been even more obvious when he'd held Shawn close to him in the water.

Trent coughed into his fist and inclined his head away from the man he hadn't been able to push from his mind since the first time they'd met. Trent couldn't even remember how they'd ended up talking at the event, yet he easily recalled how he hadn't been able to stop caressing the officer with his stare the entire time. He was sure Shawn had noticed. Walking away had been the only answer. He would have been too weak otherwise. It didn't matter how attracted he was to Shawn, he didn't need another cop in his life. Never again.

"Ready to pack up here?"

Trent was pulled from his reverie by his driver, Lee.

"Yeah. We're done."

He chanced another peek in the direction of Shawn and saw that his partner and one of the sergeants from the area command were with him. It was none of his business and he knew Shawn could take care of himself, yet he couldn't help the urge inside him to verify that he was being properly attended to.

"Trent! Are we rolling or what?"

He balled up the blanket the medic had handed him and made a mental note to return it to the hospital the following day. The evening heat had done a fine job of drying the outer layer of his uniform, but he couldn't say the same for his tighty-whities. They were chafing him in the most annoying—and potentially embarrassing—of ways. He boosted himself into the passenger side of the engine and Lee eased the massive truck out onto the Boulevard, heading south for a quick drive back to the nearby station.

"So, saved a cop, huh?" Lee chuckled. "Now that we've one upped them, they're gonna want a rematch."

Trent shook his head the way he always did when he was perplexed by the things people said. He shook his head a lot.

"I was doing my job, and so was he. It's not his fault the lush he was trying to rescue was easily two hundred fifty, sixty pounds or more. I'm surprised he did as well as he did. Although it's rather apparent he works out a lot."

Shit.

"I see. This is becoming more interesting all the time. And how would you know this rather personal bit of information, Lieutenant Marshall?"

It was a good bet he would be dizzy by the end of the night from all the head shaking. "It's rather simple. I had my arms around his torso when I pulled him from the water."

"Yeah, and your hand on his ass. That was subtle."

He fought the compelling urge to spit out his response. "I was assisting in extracting him from the lake."

Lee nodded, pursing his lips as he did. "Yeah, that's one way you could put it. Another way would be that you were checking out how much of a workout his ass gets." Lee dissolved into spasms of laughter as he turned right onto Harmon Avenue.

Sometimes he wished he'd been more discreet in coming out to his fellow team members. It had been a practical decision for him. He had wanted it out of the way so there wouldn't be any annoying inquiries or rumors. He didn't have the patience for that kind of shit. But truthfully, no one was safe when it came to possible romantic prospects. The new guy, Ronnie, had been ribbed mercilessly over one of the ER nurses at the University Medical Center he'd had a crush on. It had gotten to the point where the kid had been terrified to go anywhere near the hospital. Fortunately, Ronnie's potential paramour hadn't been intimidated by a bunch of immature public servants and had approached Ronnie instead.

After arriving back at the station, showering and changing into dry clothes, Trent headed to the kitchen to grab a bite. They'd had to jet out of there so fast when the call to the Bellagio had come in, there hadn't been an opportunity to do anything other than turn the oven off and leave their planned chicken dinner to fester on its own. He opened the metal door and was dismayed at the sight of the shriveled pieces. He gingerly picked one up and noted that it had solidified into an inedible dried-up lump. Lee sidled up to him and examined the remains.

"I don't think this one can be saved."

Trent grunted. He was a man of few words. Literally. Why jabber on endlessly when most subjects required no more than a couple of well-picked phrases?

"I'll fry up a couple burgers."

Lee seemed to consider, then reject the idea. "That's okay, I'll just grab myself a ham sandwich."

They went about the business of fixing themselves something to eat. The other two guys who had been out on the call were still taking care of the engine. Trent and Lee had handled it the previous time, so it was their turn. The medics were in the garage with them taking care of their own truck.

The common area was comprised of a long counter with cabinets on one end where the kitchen was. Alongside it were the appliances. There was enough room for two or three men to function comfortably at the same time and still have room for an eight-person dining table. Beyond that was a ten by ten square piece of carpeting which was topped with a sofa and two easy chairs. Of course, the requisite television was located in that spot as well.

Everything was very basic and utilitarian. However, they were fortunate that Vegas' budget was rather generous in comparison to other fire agencies that Trent had visited in smaller areas. The big tourist dollars paid well, but the ten stations within a three mile radius attested to the need for strong fire and rescue support. The incident they had just returned from was a perfect example of that need.

Lee picked up a piece of ham that had escaped the confines of his bread and fallen on the plate. He popped it in his mouth, narrowing his eyes at Trent as he chewed.

Trent frowned. "Something I can help you with?"

"You sure jumped right in tonight."

"Uh huh." Trent took a healthy bite of the lean beef burger he'd prepared for himself and pointedly ignored Lee as he munched away.

"You're aware that Ben and Jamal were on scene, right?"

Trent didn't answer, he just kept eating. He made a show of carefully examining his sandwich as if it were the most interesting thing ever, before taking additional bites. Unfortunately, he was almost out of burger.

"I know you're never going to bust out with any heartfelt declarations of love…"

Trent raised both eyebrows as he locked eyes with Lee. He couldn't believe what he was hearing. As if

Lee needed to reiterate that such a thing would never happen.

"...but the way you reacted tonight... Damn. I barely had a chance to inhale and you were freaking out, and in the water."

"I don't freak out." He'd said it as he'd swiped across his mouth with a paper towel then crumpled it up, dropping it on his empty plate.

"Don't think I've forgotten how you acted around him at the blood drive. You've only ever had that look on your face when you were around Paul." Lee's voice softened. "I haven't seen it on you since he died."

The chair scraped loudly as Trent forcefully pushed it back. "I have some paperwork to finish before I head to my bunk."

"Trent, come on. Would it hurt you to have an actual conversation with me? Fuck, you'd think you hated me instead of being my buddy since our glorious days of ruling over Pahrump High." Lee crossed his arms in front of himself, glowering.

Trent pressed his lips together, hating that his friend was right. Even if soul-baring conversations amounted to one of his least favorite activities on the planet, it didn't mean he had to be a total dick to the only person he felt any sort of real bond with.

Trent sighed in resignation. "Walt and I are getting together tomorrow night. He's moved into town, thinking of settling here for good."

"And you're telling me this because...?"

"We thought we might give it a try again."

Lee threw his hands in the air before letting them land on the top of his thighs with a loud smack. "Are you high?"

"That's not amusing."

"You're right. But what is really amusing is you getting back with a guy who you told me you never loved, never did it for you that much, and who you had nothing in common with. What are you thinking?"

Trent shrugged. "He's a nice guy." Glaring at Lee, he continued, "And I don't ever remember telling you anything about him 'not doing it for me' as you so eloquently put it—as if that would ever be any of your business."

Lee snorted. "First off, I could tell. I could *really* tell once you and Paul got together. Fucking night and day." Lee cleared his throat and shifted in his seat a bit. "And besides, Walt sorta mentioned something one night when you guys got in a fight."

"What?"

Walt disclosing personal information to one of his friends would be the first topic of conversation the following night. Even if the disclosure had probably occurred four or five years earlier, it was exactly the type of thing that made him uncomfortable.

"He could tell you weren't really into him. He said there wasn't any passion."

Trent groaned. "He was probably drunk."

That had been one of their major conflicts. Trent didn't mind knocking back a couple of beers, but Walt liked to over-indulge on a regular basis and hang out at the bars almost every night. It wasn't Trent's scene, but since they'd been emailing each other recently, Walt had insisted he'd changed.

"Yeah. He was. But it doesn't change the fact that he knew you weren't feeling it, if you catch my drift."

It was time for another head shaking.

"Is there a point to all of this?"

"Officer Shawn Everly."

"Don't. I mean it. Don't."

"Why the fuck not, asshole? Are you punishing yourself or something? You're gonna try to resurrect a dead relationship that was only ever on life support anyway instead of giving someone a chance who really does it for you?"

"Give him a chance...?" Trent grunted. "We've barely spoken to one another. I don't have any idea if he'd even be interested. It's not as if we've really interacted or anything."

Lee arched an eyebrow. "You mean other than a public butt fondling."

Trent flushed. "I mean it, Lee..."

"And *I* have an idea as to how interested he is."

Trent carefully schooled his expression, focused on keeping his tone neutral.

"You have no idea what you're talking about."

Lee inclined toward him as if they were involved in a deep conspiracy.

"Oh, I think I do. I most definitely know what I'm talking about. He's not as crafty at hiding his feelings as you are 'cause he was eating you up with his gaze at the blood drive, and tonight? I thought he was gonna fucking swoon or something."

Still maintaining his composure, even as Lee's words ignited an excited flutter in his chest, Trent stared his friend down.

"He almost drowned. You're misinterpreting his behavior."

Lee covered his face with his hands before dropping them back down. "You're such an idiot. What you shoulda done was carry him to the stretcher. That would have gotten you a date like that." Lee snapped his fingers.

Trent took a deep breath then stood. "Goodnight, Lee."

Lee crossed his arms in front of himself again in seeming aggravation. "Yeah, fucking idiot all right."

After turning his back on his friend, he stomped off, grateful that his shift would be over by noon the next day. He needed a couple of days away from Lee's prying. Once he got to the room he shared with his buddy and Jamal, he plopped down on the bed. He still needed to fill out an incident report, but his head was all fucked up, his thoughts uncharacteristically jumbled.

So what if he wanted Shawn? It made no difference. He'd already sworn to himself he would never get involved with another cop ever again. Paul had been the absolute love of his life, and a disgusting excuse for a human being had snatched Paul's life away while trying to rob a casino. Even though two years had passed since his lover's death and he'd grieved the loss of the man he'd thought he would spend his life with, it didn't change one significant thing. The gut-wrenching agony that had sliced through him when he'd received the news. He hadn't known that emotional pain could cut so deep. That type of hurt was something he never wanted to experience again.

When Walt had casually inquired as to where a good area would be to move to in Vegas, it had led to a discussion of one another's romantic status. It wasn't true that he hadn't loved Walt—he merely hadn't been *in* love with him. Like he'd told Lee, Walt was a nice guy. Maybe not too ambitious, still trying to figure out what he wanted to be when he grew up, and of course, there'd been the issue with the drinking. But Walt was easygoing, steady and obviously cared about Trent. He would have a regular companion—

maybe begin to build a life with someone again. He didn't need that all-encompassing love and passion that he'd had with Paul. It hurt too much when it got ripped away.

* * * *

"You could've taken tonight off, you know."

Vicki cast her eyes around at everyone going by as they strolled down the Boulevard. Shawn did the same. It would be another hot and busy night.

"I'm totally fine, Vicki. And it's not as if I had a hot date or anything."

"That's because you're too slow."

Her statement made Shawn come to a complete stop.

"What does that mean?"

He made sure to stay close to her. They were surrounded on all sides by masses of noisy partiers and the last thing he wanted to do was shout his personal business all over the Strip. The display with Lieutenant Marshall the evening before had been mortifying enough.

She'd halted as well, but her gaze continued to flit around as she spoke. "Trent Marshall is never going to approach you. You'll need to do it for him."

Shawn gasped. "Wha—? How did you…? I mean…" He swallowed hard. Was it that obvious?

Vicki charged past him and he whirled around in time to see two guys punching it out near the curb. His first concern was for her safety, although, she had proven over and over that she could handle herself fine. Still, they weren't in a position to know whether or not either man was armed.

"Stop it, *now*."

Vicki yanked on the collar of one of the fighters, struggling to pull him back so that Shawn could wedge himself between the two men. The adrenaline was high. Both he and Vicki continued to shout at them to cease, but the men were out of control. Everything had happened so fast, there hadn't been the opportunity to request backup.

The man Vicki had grabbed elbowed her, sending her flying backwards. She landed on the sidewalk with a loud grunt. Shawn released his suspect to lunge at the one who'd pushed Vicki to the ground. Grappling with him, he managed to get him in a headlock before shoving him face first to the ground. Still he struggled madly. Chaos erupted around him with the arrival of a cruiser, sirens blaring. Two officers landed on either side of Shawn and the belligerent perp, yelling for him to stop. They each took one of the man's arms to try to force them behind is body so that they could cuff him. Shawn straightened enough to push a knee into the man's lower back so that he couldn't get away.

"Stop resisting! You're making it worse for yourself. Put your hands behind your back!"

Several grueling moments later, the three of them managed to get the enraged suspect cuffed and had hauled him to his feet. He patted his fellow officer Darren on the shoulder, and wiped his lip. When he pulled his hand away he noted there was blood. Vicki handed him a tissue and he dabbed at it.

He was still worried about the tumble she'd taken.

"You okay?"

Her normally meticulously styled hair that she kept slicked back and tied in a neat bun had become severely dislodged.

"Yeah. Banged my elbow a bit, but I'll live."

"You should get it checked out."

"Sure, Everly. I'll do that when you're getting your lip checked out."

He tried to smirk at her, but it pulled on his cut. They were both stubborn asses when it came to things like that. They spent the next thirty minutes or so wrapping up the scene, getting the information they'd need for their reports later on and keeping the crowds back. Darren and Parker would transport the suspect he and Vicki had fought and another cruiser would take the one Shawn had let go. The other officers had been able to chase him down with help from some witnesses.

Fire and Rescue came out from Station 32, but there was no engine in sight. He wanted to bust his own lip again for being so stupid as to think that Trent might be his hero once again. Vicki was right. If he wanted any action from the guy, he would have to be the one to make the first move.

Obviously, he has no clue I've been eyeing him the way he's been eyeing me.

Their sergeant who'd shown up at the scene insisted they both get checked out by the paramedics. They jointly rolled their eyes at one another and went through the motions. Once they'd finished with that, they went back to their patrol. In his peripheral vision, he noticed that Vicki was constantly stealing glances at him.

"You got something to say to me, Powell?"

"Just that you're a little slow on the uptake, Everly."

"Yeah? Any suggestions?"

"Tell him you like him and wanna get together some time."

He resisted the urge to halt completely again. He'd been testing the waters as far as being openly gay was concerned. Vicki was the first person he'd come out to since moving and she'd actually wondered why he'd even brought it up. It had been awesome.

Besides the homophobe brother, the tough and hardcore task force he'd worked for in Los Angeles had not been the place for him to be out and proud. And despite the diversity of the large city, there was a very unhealthy assortment of bigots and racists in the department. He'd been part of a macho group where he hadn't felt completely comfortable disclosing his sexuality without it impacting his career. One of his hopes for his new home was that he could live more openly.

"Maybe I will." He grinned. "Of course, I'll have to get him to stand still long enough. He sure runs off quick."

"See? Too slow."

Shawn let out a good laugh. His radio crackled and he answered the call.

"Did you get that?"

Vicki nodded. "That's the new place between Hooters and the Tropicana, right?"

"Yeah, Showstoppers. I heard the food's pretty good."

"According to that call, it sounds like the hookers are even better."

They picked up a trot to get there within a reasonable amount of time. Typically, they would have let a cruiser handle anything off the Strip, but it was a busy Saturday night and Darren and the other officers were probably still dealing with the guys they'd hauled off earlier. Run-ins with prostitutes were one of the more common issues that he and his partner faced on a nightly basis. The lure of big money and a steady stream of willing customers had women—and men—traveling from all over the country to make some quick cash. What they never took into consideration was the danger and potential for disease.

They arrived at the large restaurant and bar a little out of breath. The new establishment sported a burlesque theme and they entered through the lounge door. As soon as they appeared, a man dressed in a nineteen thirties suit, complete with a top hat, approached them.

"I've been waiting almost twenty minutes. Where've you guys been?"

He had herded them into a corner but still had to keep his voice at a raised level. The pounding show tune music was difficult to hear over.

Shawn leaned in. "We apologize. There's been a lot of activity out there tonight."

The man put a hand to his forehead and nodded. "I'm sorry, I understand. It's been unusually out of control here as well."

"What have you got?"

"Two women came in together tonight and sat at the bar. One of them I swear I recognize from when we first opened. That time we didn't trespass her, but asked her to leave. Tonight, they ordered a couple drinks, but really nursed them for a while. I'd gone in the back to get some ice for the bartender and when I came back out, one of them was sitting with a guy out in the dining area. The other one"—he indicated with a jerk of his head—"is still over there drinking and eyeing the place."

The calls about the working girls were difficult in their own unique way. Without prior knowledge, such as a previous arrest, they couldn't just march up to a woman and accuse her of being a hooker. Sometimes, an officer's presence alone would encourage a prostitute to leave or to panic and give them a reason to talk to her.

"Okay. Vicki, you wanna stay here and keep an eye on her while I have Mr…?"

"Delacorte. But you can call me Owen."

"Owen. Can you take me to the dining room? Don't point anyone out, describe her to me as we head over there, then walk with me past her table."

He nodded and led Shawn from the dark lounge area, past the kitchen and into the dining room. They entered a large open space with high ceilings and a plethora of wild and colorful decorations—most of them involving feathers and velvet. There were actual life-sized figures of voluptuous women in outlandish outfits that would have made Mae West weep with envy. The statue-like pieces were reminiscent of something that could be seen at a Disneyland attraction. The room was brightly lit and the show tunes that had been the soundtrack to the bar carried over into the restaurant.

The place was packed. He followed the manager as they weaved in and out of the patron-filled tables. He almost choked.

Trent.

And he was with a man. Somehow, he couldn't picture the masculine Trent out on a date in a burlesque-themed eatery.

Date? Shit.

Inexplicably, he got angry. Irritated. He reflexively pressed his lips together which only succeeded in breaking his cut open again.

"Dammit." He muttered to himself, swiping some blood from it.

Trent glanced up, his mouth falling open a bit. Shawn wasn't able to tear his eyes away quick enough.

Guess I'm slow at everything with this guy.

Mentally kicking himself, he refocused his attention on what he was actually supposed to be doing. Owen leaned into him right as Shawn spotted the young woman.

"That's her."

Shawn gave him a curt nod and purposely looked at a point ahead of him. She was known to them, so he needed to figure out a way to get her out of the main dining area. Fortunately, Owen guided him to the hall leading to the restrooms that were located on the other side of the dining area.

"Well?"

The manager stared at him expectantly.

"Yeah, we've arrested her before. Let me radio my partner and find out what the situation is back in the bar. Keep an eye on our girl out there and alert me if it seems like she might make a run for it."

Owen scurried back to the dining area and Shawn contacted Vicki. Once he'd confirmed that the other woman was still at the bar, they determined they would each collar their suspect and meet up in the back, behind the restaurant. Shawn alerted dispatch so that they could send a cruiser over as soon as possible if they needed a transport.

Right as he clicked off, he raised his head. He sucked in a breath at the sight of Trent ambling down the hall toward him.

Be cool.

Trent stopped in front of him, so very close. So tempting.

"What happened to your lip?"

Shawn was about to answer, but snapped his jaw shut instead.

The fuck?

Chuckling, he managed to answer. "Uh, tussle on the Strip." He furrowed his brow, perplexed. "So you came back here just to ask me that?"

"You should be more careful."

"Sure, I'll keep that in mind. I *am* a cop. Shit happens."

Trent scowled at him, crossing his arms in a defiant gesture as he did. "*Exactly*."

Shawn had to admit he was completely lost. Trent was hot and sexy, but that didn't mean he might not be one card shy of a full house. Shawn's radio crackled, offering him a respite from having to come up with something to say immediately.

"Are you out back?"

"We have a situation. There's smoke pouring from the kitchen area. I've called it in, but we've gotta get these people outta here now."

Chapter Three

Fire.

The restaurant was unbelievably packed and Trent knew they would have to move fast, especially with all the fluffy decorations the place had plastered all over. He'd been fairly stunned when Walt had insisted on coming to the eatery.

Shawn turned to him, about to speak, but Trent interrupted him.

"I heard. I'll help you clear everyone out."

Not responding, Shawn took off for the dining area and Trent followed. He was relieved to see that the smoke wasn't yet visible from the curtained area that led to the bar. It would be easier to get the patrons outside quickly and easily if there wasn't a panic.

He noted Shawn whipping his head around, obviously in search of someone. Trent was at his side.

"Who're you looking for?"

"I need the manager to shut off this damned music, but he's disappeared. It's so loud I won't be heard over it if I make a general announcement."

Trent nodded. "See if you can get one of the staff to do something about that while I go to the tables closest to the drapes. I'll get those people out first. Maybe the rest will take the hint."

"Good plan."

Right then, a theme-dressed man walked past. Shawn grabbed the arm of the server.

"I need to evacuate the restaurant. Can you shut off this music so I can make an announcement?"

The young man's eyes went wide. "Why? What's wrong?"

"It's just a precaution. There's nothing to worry about. Could you look into that for me? Hurry."

The kid nodded, clearly not convinced that he shouldn't worry. Before he could stop himself, Trent lightly grasped Shawn's elbow.

"Come help me with these tables in the meantime. There's still a chance we can get everyone to move out before you even have to make an announcement."

He tried not to notice how Shawn had tensed slightly when he'd touched his arm. Shawn nodded but had an odd look on his face.

"Don't you want to let your date know first? I can always get started over here while you do that."

Trent regarded Shawn, watching as his Adam's apple bobbed up and down a couple of times, a hint of nervousness evident.

"He's not my date. Let's get moving."

Shawn turned his back on him and approached one of the tables closest to the lounge entrance. Trent couldn't help but be impressed at how calm he was, careful to keep his voice low as he ushered a young couple from their chairs toward the front.

Trent tore his gaze away and went about encouraging additional patrons to vacate the restaurant. After a few groups of people left, there was a distinct murmur that could be heard amongst the restaurant goers. He was in the process of speaking to three elderly couples about safely exiting when he felt a grip on his arm. He glanced up to see Walt.

"What's going on? Were you just gonna leave me there?"

"Wait for me outside, Walt."

Trent moved toward the next table, the occupants already gathering their things as he did so. The message to leave seemed to have swept the room. His arm was grabbed again. This time, Trent whirled around in frustration. He'd already suspected that Walt had been drinking before he'd arrived at Showstoppers, but his behavior indicated that it was more likely than not that he had.

"Not now. Go outside."

Trent tried to turn away again, but Walt stepped in front of him.

"Who's that cop, huh? I saw the way you guys gawked at each other, you acting like you were caught where you shouldn't be. He your boyfriend? I know how you've got a thing for policemen."

"I said not *now. Leave.*"

His words had been gritted out through his teeth, heat rising to his face in barely controlled fury. Walt's own anger shone back at him, but he finally stomped off.

Lee was right. What was I thinking?

People moved hurriedly toward the propped open doors in a calm manner, and Trent was relieved that the evacuation was proceeding well. Both he and Shawn were mid-way through the dining room, herding more and more patrons out of the restaurant. A loud bang preceded a whoosh of flames. Smoke burst through the drapes as large tongues of fire rapidly consumed the velvet curtains. Screams rang out, tables and chairs toppled over and people pushed one another aside to scramble for the entrance. Trent attempted to calm those around him, but already the garish decorations around them were lit up by the searing blaze. It was time to leave.

Trent caught sight of Shawn desperately trying to stem the panic. Instead, he was shoved against a wall by a group of men as they rushed past him. Shawn winced as if he was in pain. Already amped up from his altercation with Walt and the adrenaline of the situation, seeing Shawn get manhandled set something off in him. Without thinking, he rushed over.

When he reached his side, he was aggravated to see Shawn rubbing his shoulder and grimacing as if he'd really been hurt. His eyes seemed to light up when he saw Trent.

"I think we've done as much as we can do. Let's get you out of here."

Shawn frowned. "You mean, let's both get out of here."

As if in confirmation, Trent coughed, smoke beginning to fill the room uncomfortably. "I need to verify that all the staff has vacated and that there aren't any patrons in the restrooms."

"I've got this. I'm on duty, you're not. Anyone still left behind would most likely listen to me since I'm in uniform."

Shawn choked out his last words, the smoke building at too rapid of a rate. Sirens sounded and Trent knew help had arrived. Shawn fell into a coughing fit and Trent made a split second decision. He grabbed hold of Shawn's right wrist, yanked it up while ducking his head under Shawn's arm. He pulled it back down then reached through Shawn's legs, transferring the man's wrist to his other hand. Tightening his hold, he hoisted Shawn up on his shoulder in a perfect fireman's carry and rushed to the front, the doors finally clear.

He'd expected a struggle, but he imagined he'd probably caught Shawn by surprise. Depositing him on the sidewalk away from the restaurant, he straightened up to see Shawn's enraged glare. Lee trotted past them and punched Trent in the arm as he went by. He was already in complete gear with his mask and helmet, so was unable to deliver what would likely have been some sort of sarcastic remark.

Trent cleared his throat, more confused by his own behavior than even Shawn probably was.

"We should move back further."

Shawn still appeared to be seething. "As I was *saying*, I'm on duty. I got shit to do."

With that, he marched off, seeming to pointedly ignore the bemused looks and stares of his fellow officers there helping with crowd and traffic control. Trent couldn't deny his own discomfort at what a display his actions had undoubtedly made, so he could only imagine how Shawn felt. The last thing he'd wanted to do was embarrass him, to do damage to his masculinity by inferring Shawn needed constant rescuing.

Shit.

A knee-jerk reaction. That was all it had been. However, Shawn was probably only focusing on the jerk part of it. He ducked his head, suddenly anxious to get away from the scene, away from any possible comments from anyone. There wasn't anything he could do to help, and he'd likely only be in the way. It also appeared that Walt had taken off. Carefully avoiding any eye contact and not giving in to the temptation to seek out Shawn's whereabouts, he headed down the street to the garage where he'd left his truck. He needed to go home and get his head on straight, figure out his next move. Lee had been right about another thing. He wanted Shawn more than he'd wanted anyone since Paul. He still wasn't convinced he could handle it, should chance it, but if nothing else—he should apologize to him.

Since there was a strong likelihood that Shawn would never want to have anything to do with him again, it was possible the whole thing would work itself out. Maybe he wouldn't have to stress over it. The guy was probably so pissed off at him that all hope was lost for them to ever be together anyway.

There was a tightening in his gut as he realized he did want it to work out after all. That he not only wanted Shawn Everly badly, but wanted more than just a hook up.

He was quite fucked.

* * * *

"I don't want to fucking talk about it."

It was the day after the fire at Showstoppers and Shawn had made the mistake of stopping by the station to see if there were any changes to the schedule. They were adding a few new officers to the team and there had been some hints that things might get shuffled around. His hopes that interest in the events of the past couple of nights would have faded in importance had decidedly been dashed. Almost from the moment he'd set foot in the station, he'd been subjected to crude remarks about Trent Marshall saving a damsel in distress and other stupid observations regarding Trent's hands on his ass.

He'd ducked into the break room to escape them all and Vicki had followed him in. She'd been on her way out of the building after being there for the same reason as him, but had turned on her heels and chased after him instead. He was kicking it in there with her in an attempt to regroup before he finished his final walk of shame out the door.

Part of what bothered him was that he couldn't tell if his fellow officers were mocking him good-naturedly or if there was a tinge of homophobia involved. He hadn't been around any of them long enough to know one way or another. At least he knew Vicki was cool. But that still didn't mean he wanted to talk about anything regarding Trent.

"You wanna grab a coffee?"

"And not talk?" He was being a tad bitchy and he knew it. "Sorry. I might stay in here until everyone leaves."

"You're overreacting."

One thing he really liked about Vicki was how direct she was. She didn't offer long drawn out expositions on everything. She cut to the chase. He responded well to people who were like that. They seemed more honest.

"I disagree. The little performance our associates gave out there is all the proof I need to verify my feelings."

She shrugged. "Who gives a shit about them?" She paused as if she were carefully forming her thoughts before sharing them. "Look, I've been through it with a lot of these dickwads, I know how it feels. You have to remember there are the good ones too, like Darren and Parker."

"Whaddya mean, you know how it feels?"

She seemed to get along with everyone really well, and he'd been impressed from the moment he'd gotten there with how well-respected she was. He wasn't sure what she was trying to say.

"When I started, I got a lot of flak. Some of the guys threw around some passive aggressive bullshit since they couldn't openly say they didn't want a female partner—or that they thought a woman cop would be too weak to handle herself. My former partner—the one you replaced—helped me out. The best advice he gave me was to never let them know that they bothered you. It took a while, but I proved myself through my work and my attitude. No one fucks with me now."

"It's all so lame."

She shrugged again. "Yuppers. It is." Stretching, she looked at her watch. "So, since you won't get a coffee with me, I'll leave you with one final comment."

Shawn groaned. At least he knew that anything she had to say about his situation would not only be sincere but would be said from a place of real concern.

"Okay. Have at it."

"The man wants you. Bad. Fucking do something about it already."

She rose from her chair then grabbed her wallet from the table. Right as she turned to leave, two of the officers who'd been giving him a hard time earlier peeked around the door.

"Hey, Everly. Your boyfriend is here looking for you."

They both broke into laughter. The other one piped in.

"Yeah, he said he needs to make sure your ass is okay."

He and Vicki exchanged glances. She was right—they were monkeys.

"I would've been disappointed if he didn't make sure it was okay."

They stopped in mid-guffaw and frowned at each other. The first one turned back to him.

"I don't get it."

"Obviously."

He rose from his chair and brushed past them, noting Vicki's satisfied grin before he left the room.

Now I have to face Trent.

That part of his grand exit could've been thought through better. He was still insanely angry at the man, yet a new emotion crept up on him—excitement. It was too confusing, so he focused on one thing. Getting out of the station. The last thing he was about to do—regardless of how he felt about Trent—was to stand there in the lobby and yak about anything personal.

No point in handing out the ammunition for free.

He inhaled sharply the moment he saw Trent. Their eyes locked and Shawn knew he was toast. Yeah, he was still pissed off at Trent, but that did nothing to change how incredibly drawn to him he was.

In an attempt to maintain some level of composure, Shawn cast his gaze down as he made his way from behind the counter. Peripherally, he saw Trent move toward him. Shawn kept up a steady pace as he made his way to the door.

"Shawn, I'd like to speak with you for a moment..."

Never slowing, Shawn pressed forward. He wasn't about to stop and have a conversation of any nature while they were still inside the building.

"Shawn?"

Fucking get a clue.

As he stepped from the icy air of the station into the instantaneous blast of August heat, he finally slowed. The moment Trent was outside, Shawn turned his head slightly—still unable to meet Trent's eyes—and subtly gestured for him to follow. He remained blissfully silent as they walked to the garage where Shawn had his car parked.

At last they reached his Toyota Rav4 in the shade of the parking structure. It basically meant that the temperature was probably only ninety instead of over a hundred. But at least they weren't in the direct sun. Shawn spun around to face Trent. This time, he did look right at Trent—and was immediately sorry. They were within two feet of one another. Alone. No immediate emergencies occurring. It was definitely a first for all three things at once. It made him hard.

"I apologize for last night."

Shawn thought about tearing into the guy but didn't have the energy all of a sudden.

Must be the heat.

He decided to have a discussion with him instead. Somewhere buried underneath the anger he held against Trent Marshall for the way he'd behaved the night before was the desire to get their obvious mutual attraction out in the open. Deal with it one way or the other.

"What you did was incredibly humiliating."

Trent nodded, still holding his gaze. "I realize that. That's why I wanted to apologize to you."

The man was not the most talkative thing on two legs. It didn't seem like he wanted to add to his statement, yet he gave no indication he was about to leave either.

"Then why the hell did you do it?"

Shawn watched in fascination as a whole buffet of emotions seemed to flit across Trent's face. His muscles bunched slightly as he tensed up, clenching his jaw and balling his fists. Shawn couldn't even begin to imagine what could be so distressing about what had happened the night before, especially since Trent wasn't the one who'd been embarrassed in front of all their peers.

"Well?"

"I was concerned for your safety."

"Um, yeah. And I appreciate the thought. But it seemed rather over the top, don't you think? I mean, you just apologized for it, right?"

Shawn noted the sweat beading on Trent's forehead then tracked a drop as it trailed down the side of his face. He swiped at his own forehead, the heat getting to that point where it would begin to suck the life out of him until all he wanted to do was take a nap for the next fifty years.

"Have you had lunch?"

Shawn resisted the urge to laugh. Trent was difficult to follow. But since he'd wanted to find a way to approach the guy about them getting together anyway, Trent's invite was perfect—except for one small detail.

"We don't have to go anywhere around here, do we?"

Trent made a face as though he'd smelled something really bad. "God, no. There's an old diner about five miles from here that I go to a lot. No one I know ever shows up there. It's a great place to have some peace and a decent meal."

"Perfect. In that case, I'd love to get lunch."

Trent nodded, still staring at him with his intense blue eyes.

"Why don't we ride together in my truck?"

Shawn chuckled. "Why? Are we having a date?"

"Yes."

Stopping mid-chuckle, Shawn couldn't help but let his jaw drop. Straightforward was too mellow a term to describe Trent Marshall.

"Oh. I see."

"Then let's get going."

Trent's deep, growly voice gave Shawn the shivers under normal circumstances. When he used it to order him around, it threatened to make him come right then and there.

"S-sure."

Trent pierced him with one more steely gaze then jerked his head to the other side of the garage before turning and heading that way. Shawn followed after him, fighting the sensation that he had just been brought to heel. Oddly, it didn't bother him. Something about giving himself over to Trent suddenly held a lot of appeal.

Perfect. The voracious heat has melted my brains.

His dick was doing remarkably well however. All it seemed to care about was that he and Trent were apparently going on an officially sanctioned date. It wasn't as romantic as a burlesque restaurant, but it was a start. He snorted. Trent peered over his shoulder, no doubt wondering what Shawn had thought was so funny. Thinking about the restaurant did bring something up for Shawn though.

They reached Trent's newer red Ford F-150, and after unlocking the passenger side, Trent opened the door for him. He put one foot on the step to lift himself inside and had a flash that Trent would palm his ass again. It didn't happen and he wasn't sure how he felt about that.

Once Trent climbed into the driver's side, he started up the engine and they were on their way. He noted how Trent would glance at him occasionally, almost as if he were checking to see if he was really there. Typically, Shawn didn't consider himself to be tongue-tied, but he'd been so surprised by the insta-date situation, and he was still in the midst of processing it.

Date. That's right.

"Um, last night. That guy you were with. Not that it's any of my business, but you said he wasn't your date. I just want to clarify that we're not sneaking around behind someone's back. I'm not into that."

"Good. Me neither."

"So…you guys are just friends…or something?"

Shawn watched as Trent seemed to be working through his thoughts. His jaw was clenched and he stared straight forward, his eyebrows pulled together.

"He's an ex from a while back. He wants to start up again, but I've decided I don't."

"Oh."

Shawn had the impression that Trent didn't really want to talk about his ex anymore, so he dropped it for the time being. It was clear to him that Trent wasn't a gabby kind of a guy, so he would likely have to get his info from him in bite sized pieces. As with Vicki though, he appreciated that the man was a straight shooter. He didn't anticipate having to sift through a lot of bullshit.

They arrived at the diner on the other side of the interstate and although a little run down, when they stepped inside Shawn was assailed with the aroma of homemade food. He could see why Trent would want to make it a regular destination. They sat in a booth across from one another in the very back, the place thankfully almost empty. Shawn was thrown when the waitress only handed a menu to him. He lifted his eyebrows at Trent.

"I already know what's on that."

"Any recommendations?"

"I'd have to know what you like."

"You could always ask."

Trent considered him, his eyes narrowing a little.

"Okay. I'm asking."

"As much as I love comfort food once in a while, I tend to eat fairly healthy."

"I like all the salads, but they make a damn good Cobb. I also like the turkey and avocado sandwich."

Shawn glanced over the well-worn menu, the plastic laminate peeling away on parts of the edges. "Hmm. Actually, the turkey avocado sounds excellent. I think I'll go for that."

The server returned. Trent gently took the menu from Shawn and handed it to her.

"Two turkey avocado sandwiches, Lora." He looked at Shawn. "Drink?"

"Iced tea, no lemon."

He turned back to Lora. "I'll have the same with iced tea too, but bring lemon with mine."

"Sure thing, Trent."

After she walked away, they were back to staring at one another. This time when heat rose to his face, it had nothing to do with the temperature.

"You still haven't told me why you threw me over your shoulder like a caveman last night."

He wants forthright. I'll give him forthright.

Trent made a small grunt. "That wasn't my intent."

"Fine. What was your intent then?"

Trent cast his eyes down and fiddled with the spoon lying on his paper napkin. Lora came by with their drinks. Trent thanked her and waited until she'd walked away again before speaking.

"How's your lip?"

"*What*? Are you nuts? Why can't you answer a simple question?"

Shawn's frustration grew. Trent could blurt most things out without hesitation, yet this one topic he kept dancing around.

What the hell?

Squirming in the booth, Trent clasped his hands in front of him. Shawn noted how white his knuckles became from the obvious tension-filled grip Trent had on them.

"I lost my lover, my partner and best friend while he was in the line of duty." Trent met his gaze. "He was on the Homeland Security SAT team and was the first one on the scene of a robbery at a casino. He was shot in the head and died instantly. When I saw you in trouble at the Bellagio—saw you almost drown—it was too much..." Trent lowered his eyes for a moment as if to gather himself before raising them again and continuing. "I like you a lot. Last night was uncalled for, but I want you to understand that it came from a place of concern. All I could think of was getting you to safety."

Holy shit.

"Oh God, Trent, I'm so sorry. I had no idea."

Shawn was taken aback by the revelation. He wished Vicki had warned him. She had to know, didn't she?

"Don't worry about last night. It was just my stupid pride that was hurt." He cleared his throat. "And I really appreciate what you did at the Bellagio. Truth be told, I was scared shitless. I actually thought I was a goner."

He looked at Trent with as much sincerity as he could muster.

"Thank you for that. I mean it."

Trent dipped his chin in acknowledgment. Lora approached the table with their food and they went about eating.

"Mmm. Thanks for the suggestion. This is really good."

Shawn spied what he was sure was an actual smile on Trent's face. It hadn't occurred to him until that moment that he never saw Trent smile much. When he did, it wasn't a big toothy one but more of an amused sideways smirk. It fit him.

Trent put the second half of his sandwich down then took a swallow of his tea sans straw. He set down his glass. "When's your next day off?"

An unexpected swell of giddiness surged through Shawn. Trent would only be asking such a thing if he wanted them to get together.

"I have the next couple days off. Why?"

"Good. I have tomorrow off then don't go back in until noon the following day. Have you been to Red Rock Canyon since you moved here?"

"Actually, I haven't. I've wanted to check it out, though. I'd love to take some pictures there. It's a bit of a hobby for me."

Trent nodded at him. "I know."

Shawn straightened. "You do?"

"I asked Vicki about you."

He arched his eyebrows. "You're kidding."

"That bother you?"

He considered it. "When did you talk to her?"

"Before I saw you at the station."

Shawn pressed his lips together, frowning. No wonder she'd been so pushy about him talking to Trent.

"I don't know if I'm bothered as much as surprised."

It's actually kinda hot. And here I thought I was going to have to go after him.

"We gettin' together then?"

"Sure. But is this someplace you want to go to also?"

Trent stared at him in the way that made Shawn feel very exposed.

"It's one of my favorite places around here. She also said you enjoyed hiking. So do I."

"Jesus. Did she write an essay or something?" He shifted in his seat when Trent didn't say anything. "We'd have to get there pretty early to get any hiking in before it gets too hot."

"I'll pick you up at six in the morning. We can grab some breakfast then do some hiking. After that, we should go to the visitor center. There're some interesting things you might like to photograph, rust colored striped rocks or Mojave Max, their desert tortoise."

"Mojave Max, huh?"

Shawn exhaled slowly, relaxing in the booth. He had the oddest sensation of being completely at ease with Trent. Despite all the avoidance Trent had done and the weirdness of the previous couple of days, there was a marked connection between them. They melded together well. He supposed spending all day with only one another to talk to and going somewhere completely removed from their normal everyday lives would be a good test. If their spark was no more than a simple physical reaction, they would find out quick enough.

But he doubted that was the case. He was sure there was something more than simple lust occurring. However, if things went the way he was certain they would, he had a feeling there would be a lot more physical activity than hiking going on between them.

"Sounds great. Red Rock Canyon it is."

* * * *

Dawn was breaking the horizon as Trent pulled up to Shawn's apartment house. After he parked the truck, he paused for a moment, gripping the steering wheel. There was a tightening in his abdomen, a sensation he hadn't felt for years. Elation. Desire. Warmth toward another human being.

I'm alive and Shawn's right here.

Closing his eyes, he thought of his beautiful former lover—how Paul had filled his life with so much love.

"Thank you. I'll always love and miss you, but it's time to move on."

He took a deep breath and exited the vehicle, nervousness worming its way in with his other emotions. Crossing the street, he noted that the newer building Shawn lived in had closed glass doors that could only be opened with a security code. *Good.* He found Shawn's name on the digital screen and tapped the numbers. He was buzzed in right away, Shawn never verifying who it was. Frowning at the screen, he grabbed the door before the noise stopped. Shawn's apartment was on the ground floor and he wound his way along a cement path that boasted stones embedded within. The whole property was meticulously kept with an interesting variety of cacti and succulents. The early hour meant that the surroundings were quiet, peaceful. When he reached

Shawn's place, he saw that the door was slightly ajar. He knocked lightly and heard Shawn call out from somewhere within.

"Come in!"

He took another deep breath, his heart rate accelerating. There were crazy scenarios running through his mind of someone who had a vendetta against the cop following him to his home, Shawn buzzing him in without even verifying who it was, walking right through the open door…

"Good morning. Sorry, just getting the rest of my gear together."

"How did you know it was me outside?"

Shawn lifted his head from an open backpack perched on a small kitchen table. He'd been in the process of stuffing a T-shirt and sunscreen inside.

"Who else would be buzzing me at the crack of dawn?"

Shawn had a grin on his face and Trent felt like a jerk. Again.

"I…I mean what if it hadn't been? What if it was someone who…?" He knew he shouldn't finish the sentence.

The grin Shawn had been sporting fell and was replaced by an irritated grimace.

"Trent. It's six in the morning. The day has barely begun. Could we not start off like this?"

He winced. Shawn was right. If only he could get the pounding in his heart to subside—the insistent reminder that so many things could go wrong in an instant—he would be fine.

Enjoy the day. Don't overthink, overreact.

"Of course. I apologize. Let me help you with that." He reached for Shawn's pack.

"Thanks, but I got it. I have some extra bottled waters in the fridge, plus some protein bars. You want me to bring 'em?"

"Good. We can add them to what I packed up."

Shawn turned to step into the small kitchen right off the sitting area where the table was. "Oh yeah? What'd you bring?"

"Made some sandwiches, threw in some fruit, some Gatorade."

"Perfect. Can't wait."

Shawn reappeared, grin intact, his arms full. Trent lurched forward to grab a couple of bottles in danger of leaping from Shawn's grasp. He got a hold of them, but not before their limbs and hands had collided.

Fuck. Hard already.

He quickly twisted away to avoid Shawn's scrutiny—or his reaction.

"How about an omelet for breakfast? I know a place on the way out of town where they have a whole mess of options."

Trent was careful to keep himself angled so that he didn't completely face Shawn.

Shawn cleared his throat. "Lead the way." He'd said it softly.

Trent chanced a look, allowed himself to lock eyes with Shawn. It was right there. A true connection, something more than just desire. As much as he'd been afraid of it from the very moment he'd met the sweetly sexy cop, he wanted to accept the gift that stood before him. The chance to start anew and have it be really good again.

Once they'd tossed everything into the space behind the front seat, they were on their way. There had been many, many hours he'd spent at Red Rock Canyon over the years. After he'd lost Paul, he'd gone there quite a bit to achieve a small portion of serenity. It had been healing for him. He hoped it could morph into something new through sharing it with Shawn. He wanted to share everything with Shawn.

* * * *

The vistas were amazing, the rock formations striking. Shawn felt bad that he kept stopping every few minute to take pictures, but he couldn't help it. He was ecstatic that Trent had brought him to such a spectacular place for their first outing together—and that he'd been continually treated to the sight of Trent's rippling quads that were on display below his shorts. His ass bunching under his thin khaki shorts had been rather delightful as well. It was awesome letting Trent take the lead.

"If all my picture taking is annoying you, tell me to stop." He laughed lightly. "I don't wanna bore you."

"I'm not bored."

Trent had maintained his intense gaze on him all morning. It was a look Shawn doubted he could ever get enough of, the sort of look that made a man want to fall into a spontaneous orgasm. He covered the smile forming on his lips at the thought, the visual cracking him up on the inside. It appeared he hadn't been entirely successful at hiding his mirth.

"What's so funny?"

There wasn't the slightest chance he was going to blurt out what he'd actually been thinking. He settled for an approximation of the truth. "I'm really enjoying myself. Thanks for bringing me here. It was a good call."

There was a slight pull at the corners of Trent's mouth. "It's not much farther to the water basin. Can't promise how full it'll be this time of year. But it'd be a good place to rest, maybe have a bite."

"Sounds good."

They hiked along, picking their way over areas filled with large boulders all jumbled together, the ever-present reddish cast blending in with the soft beige tones. They headed up a gradual incline and once they'd cleared it, there was a big open area below the massive rock formation on which they stood. A natural ledge of sorts ran along the side of one of the weather smoothed cliffs that led to the banks of the rather depleted water hole.

"Let's work our way down there. There's a couple spots we can sit and catch a bit of shade."

Shawn followed Trent, careful to walk slightly angled to the side to avoid having his feet slip out from under him. When they reached the bottom, he saw another couple relaxing farther over. The man and woman both nodded their way, and they returned the acknowledgment. It was barely nine in the morning and the few hikers who were willing to brave the desert in the summertime knew to get their excursions in either before or after the worst of the heat.

After taking off their packs, they leaned against the smooth rock face, stretching their legs before them. It was the closest he and Trent had sat to one another, only a few inches separating them from touching.

"If the water were any higher, we would've had to scooch up to keep our feet from getting wet."

"Scooching, huh?" Shawn chuckled.

He watched as Trent tilted his head back to gaze up at the deep blue sky, squinting behind his sunglasses. He was leaning back on his elbows.

"You got something against scooching?"

"No, scooching's good. Real good."

Trent made a small grunting noise then lolled his head toward Shawn.

"I'm enjoying myself quite a bit too."

There had been a thick growl to Trent's tone and Shawn was desperate for a kiss. He knew he was really desperate for a lot more, but he could start with some lip-locking.

The couple that had been there when they arrived was gathering their things and looked to be about ready to leave.

If I'm really lucky, we'll be alone for a little while.

The four of them acknowledged one another again, and the couple climbed up the face of the rock to the trail above. Right as Shawn was about to comment on them being alone, Trent cut him off.

"Finally."

Trent's cupped his strong hand on Shawn's cheek, guiding him to his mouth. As soon as Trent's lips captured his, he melted into the kiss, surprised at how it could be so commanding and so gentle at the same time. Trent kept the control, dropping his hand to brush Shawn's arm, then slowly lowering it to rest on his waist. With minimal pressure he encouraged him closer, and Shawn rolled his body until their chests touched.

As the passion in the kiss grew, they struggled to get nearer, Shawn ignoring the unforgiving rock. It was apparent Trent was ignoring it as well. He reached around Shawn's neck and shoulders and pulled him flush to the hard planes of his body, lowering his other hand more until he grasped Shawn's ass.

Oh God.

Trent's tongue was a wonder as he used it to explore the cavern of Shawn's mouth. Each time Trent pulled away then dipped in deeply, Shawn gave a little more of himself—gave himself over to Trent's demands. It was the first time in a long while that he could remember making out the way they were doing. They both knew they wouldn't—couldn't—take it any further right then, and that was okay.

Right as they began to grind against one another, Trent pulled back, as breathless as Shawn was. He loosened his hold somewhat, petting Shawn's face, brushing an errant strand of hair back from Shawn's forehead. Trent continued to look him over as if he were examining him, seeing him for the first time. He ran a thumb across Shawn's bottom lip then draped his hand softly over his waist, letting it rest there.

"Very nice."

Trent had a completely contented expression as he'd said it. It was startling to Shawn how easy it was for them to gaze into one another's eyes. He'd never realized before how intimate an action it was, how close it made him feel to Trent. He couldn't honestly remember ever noticing such a thing about any other man he'd been with. Of course, Trent wasn't any other man.

"Yes. Nice."

Trent placed more light kisses across his face, ending with a peck on his nose.

"I'd like to continue this later at my house."

Shawn nodded. "Whatever you want."

These was a curl to one side of Trent's mouth. "Oh, *I want.*"

Shawn wasn't aware that he'd ever gulped before, but he was certain that was what he'd just done.

That fucking deep voice.

The sound alone made Shawn want to drop his pants and bend over.

A child's loud screech above their heads alerted them that they were about to have company, so they reluctantly let each other go. They rolled back to their previous positions. After snacking on a couple of granola bars and rehydrating, they got their things ready. Trent pushed up from the rock and Shawn allowed himself to take in the glorious view of his rippling muscles as he stood. Letting his gaze travel up the length of Trent's body, he stopped when he met Trent's eyes.

Trent had a self-satisfied grin. "Soon."

He held out his hand and Shawn took it, the brute strength in Trent's grip remarkable as he yanked him up. Once he was on his feet, Trent grabbed his upper arm and twisted Shawn a little so that his backside was hidden from the view of the family nearby. Shawn startled when his ass was brushed quickly but forcefully.

"You had a lot of dirt."

Trent gave his arm a squeeze then let go. How could such a small gesture make his heart so full? Why did every miniscule thing Trent did or said have him practically breathless? He was almost thirty-two years old and he felt like a kid falling in love for the first time.

Love? Oh nononononono.

"Here, have some more water. You're still sweating quite a bit."

As if water was going to solve the crush of emotions surging through him. He took the bottle Trent offered and drank several small swallows. He was certain that all that was occurring was a strong dose of lust and loneliness. The sense of being cherished and cared for was in there somewhere, but he chose to temporarily ignore it.

After screwing the top back on the water, he reached behind himself to put the bottle away in his pack, but Trent took it and did it for him. After Trent had zipped it up, he ghosted his hand across Shawn's cheek then let it rest on his shoulder.

"Better?"

Shawn nodded shakily, not sure if he could trust his voice to come out as anything more than a squeak.

"Okay, but the temps are rising, so let me know if you need to stop."

He thought about grousing that he wasn't a child and could take care of himself, but found that he didn't want to. There'd never been a time in his life where he'd wanted a man to be protective toward him, to care so damn much. But he wanted that with Trent.

The rest of their time at the park was filled with an easy companionship laced with an undercurrent of desire. Once it became too hot to explore on the rocks any more, Trent had led him to the Visitor's Center. There was a lot of interesting info about the area and the rock formations as well as some great views to photograph. He'd even managed to sneak in a few shots of Trent when he wasn't looking. It had been a great day. He'd loved everything about it—even Mojave Max.

* * * *

It wouldn't help his nerves to dwell too much on things, on Shawn. It was especially perplexing as he wasn't prone to nerves. However, there was something so intoxicating about the sweet cop that it had hooked him in and wouldn't let him loose. He supposed that was the way of things. Not necessarily love—he was much too practical to believe that. But whenever he looked at Shawn he saw life. He saw a chance.

The truck radio was tuned to a local classic rock station that he'd been playing since they'd left the park. It wasn't much of a drive back to town, but the heat could take it out of the heartiest of men. He glanced to the side and saw that Shawn's head was lowered. Trent grinned to himself when Shawn jerked it back up in a vain attempt to stay awake.

Why is he so fucking cute?

Trent pulled into the driveway of his small home in Henderson just south of Vegas. He'd only had the place for a year, but the quieter city had been a nice change from being so close to the madness of central Vegas.

"Shawn, we're here."

He straightened up with a start, giving his head a little shake. "God, sorry. You wanna come in?" Shawn stretched and looked around in confusion. "Wait. Where are we?"

Trent had to chuckle. "I kidnapped you. We're at my place."

"Oh, okay." He still had a slightly puzzled expression.

"I promised you later, remember?"

Shawn turned to him with a wide smile. "Yeah, I remember."

"Then let's get you inside and cool you off before I heat you back up again."

A delightful flush filled Shawn's cheeks and Trent had the bizarre urge to scoop him up from the passenger side and carry him into the house. But given his most recent experience carrying Shawn, he thought it best that he save it for another time.

Yes. Another time.

They went through the requisite motions of carrying everything into the house, Trent watching as Shawn curiously eyed the interior of his place. It had been a big step for Trent to leave his old house behind—the one he'd shared with Paul. The change had been good and he was proud of his home.

"Do you want the cooler in the kitchen?"

Trent glanced up from the hall closet where he'd just placed his hiking boots.

"I can get that, Shawn."

"Trent, seriously. I'm capable of carrying a cooler."

He stopped in mid-gait. "Of course. I didn't mean anything by it. I just don't want you to have to go to any trouble. You're my guest."

Shaking his head, Shawn gave him a smirk. "Kitchen?"

Running a hand through his scruffy, sweat coated hair, Trent nodded. "Over here."

He led Shawn through the open living room that boasted sliding glass doors looking out on a covered patio and small patch of lawn, a Jacuzzi tub at one side. They stepped into the small dining room, the long kitchen to the right. Shawn set the blue and white container on the sand colored tile of the counter.

He glanced around. "This is really nice. I like the deep greens, the dark woods."

Shawn paused then faced him, too beautiful for Trent to believe he was real.

"Outdoor colors." Shawn swallowed, his edginess clear.

Trent gazed at him, took in everything that was Shawn and thanked the universe that he stood before him, in his home. The magic that had been simmering between them all day bubbled to the surface. Trent held out his hand and Shawn stepped forward to silently take it.

With their fingers laced together, he guided Shawn down the hall past the dining area, into the master bedroom at the far end. As soon as they were inside the room, Trent turned, pulling Shawn to him. He grabbed the back of his head with one hand and his ass with the other. Plunging into his mouth, he took what he wanted. It wasn't gentle like it had been back at the rocks, he wanted to claim Shawn, demand that he give him everything.

Shawn opened up, clutching at his shoulder blades. They both ground against one another, and the need that washed over Trent engulfed him. In between hungry kisses, they tilted their heads at varying angles, moving in then pulling away. It was a joyous battle as their tongues swept through one another's mouth, Shawn surrendering himself to Trent's passion. The urgency built, their breathing accelerating. Trent ran his hands possessively over Shawn's body, Shawn clinging to him. He broke their kiss but didn't let go.

"Let's take this to the shower."

Gasping, Shawn nodded. "Good idea."

He noted the startled look on Shawn's face as he tugged at the hem of Shawn's shirt while simultaneously unbuttoning the top of his shorts with one hand.

"Help me out."

Shawn nodded again with a somewhat dazed expression and pulled the tee over his head as Trent yanked his shorts down. He wrapped his arms around Shawn's thighs to keep him from tumbling over, manipulating him the way he needed him. Glad that Shawn had left his boots in the entryway, he was able to bring the dusty socks along for the ride as he removed the remainder of Shawn's clothing. At last Shawn was naked.

The way he should always be in my home.

If he hadn't already been sporting an erection of steel, the thought of Shawn's constant nudity would have done it. He stood, noting the light blush across Shawn's torso, in his face. His chest rose and fell rapidly. But it was his hard rosy crowned cock that drew Trent's gaze. He was average length, but thick and gorgeous. Moisture leaked from the tip, even as it seemingly twitched of its own accord. Trent couldn't keep his hands off.

Shawn drew in a sharp breath as soon as Trent encircled his stiff column of flesh. He licked the side of Shawn's neck, tasting the salt of his dried sweat. As he softly stroked him, he wanted nothing more than to bend Shawn over the end of the bed and plunge into his sweet ass, but he would take his time. They still had the rest of the day and evening, it was early yet and he planned on savoring their first sexual experience together.

Letting go, he steadied Shawn then gave him a brief kiss. The urge he'd experienced in the truck came back. Before he could let his thoughts intrude, he gathered Shawn in his arms to carry him into the en suite bathroom. He'd expected resistance, but was pleasantly surprised when Shawn relaxed in his embrace. Once they were next to the shower stall that was separate from the sunken tub, he set him down.

"I promise to only do that when we're alone."

"Deal."

He was relieved to see that Shawn didn't appear miffed in any way. His dick certainly appeared happy enough.

Trent readied the water, but continuously stole peeks of Shawn's stunning body. It looked even better than it had felt. Defined abs and hip lines, strong arms and legs proportioned wonderfully, a nice muscular butt—everything he'd dreamed Shawn would be. He returned his attention to the shower. Even though they'd been in the blistering heat all morning and part of the afternoon, he didn't want to make it too cool. He had central air conditioning that kept his home at a comfortable temperature.

Trent extended his hand again and Shawn took it, but inclined his head in apparent confusion, no doubt wondering why Trent hadn't undressed yet.

"Don't you want to join me?"

"Of course I do. Step inside. I'll be right back."

Shawn did as he'd been told and Trent ducked quickly out of the bathroom and jogged down the hall. He'd been brash enough to purchase lube and condoms the night before, but hadn't followed through with putting them in the nightstand. Once he'd brought the items home, he'd thought that maybe he was being too presumptuous. He'd clearly been mistaken.

They were still on the counter in the plastic bag from the pharmacy. Shawn had set the cooler right next to it and it had reminded Trent they were there. He grabbed what he needed and scurried back to the bedroom, tearing apart the cardboard container that imprisoned the lube as he went. Once he'd put everything away, he frantically yanked off his own clothing, anxious to be skin to skin with Shawn.

He entered the bathroom, light steam beginning to fill the area. Pulling the glass door open to the shower stall, he then stepped inside, immediately gathering a soapy Shawn to his body.

"Oh, Jesus."

Shawn sounded breathless.

"Anything wrong?"

"Fuck no. You feel so good."

Trent chuckled, leaning down to give Shawn a deep kiss. He clutched his hair on either side of his head, reveling in the scrape of Shawn's afternoon stubble across his cheek, on his upper lip. The water surrounded them, soothing Trent, some of the suds from Shawn that hadn't been washed away transferring to his skin. They slid against one another, using their hands to explore the planes of their bodies, stealing touches between their legs, their ass cheeks. Trent was in heaven.

He could tell how relaxed Shawn was. Although he wanted to believe it was all because he was so comfortable in his home and with him, he knew some of it had to be from the soothing warm water. Shawn had already been drowsy from the heat and Trent thought it might be good for them to take a nap—to build up some energy for what Trent hoped would be a marathon fucking session later on.

Breaking free from Shawn just enough so that he could remove the cake of soap from the shower caddy, he rubbed it between his hands. He was about to reach down to wash his cock and balls when Shawn grabbed his wrist.

"Let me."

He didn't believe in degrees of hardness, but Shawn was testing that belief. It was as if every drop of blood in his body had pooled in the one location in his shaft that was gloriously pressed against Shawn's stomach.

Once Shawn had soaped up, he gave the bar back to Trent. Wedging one hand between their bodies to tend to Trent's dick and sac, he used the other to slide in his crease. Trent moaned at the contact and the way Shawn's fingers slipped across his flesh, the sensation of being thoroughly administered to so gratifying. From his taut nipples to between his toes, Shawn cleaned every part of him. He stood then tipped his head back before moving in to take Trent's mouth in a greedy kiss. Trent grabbed Shawn's hair and gently pulled his head back.

"I'm going to suck you to sleep."

Shawn sputtered laughter. "You're going to what?"

"Can you stay here tonight?"

Trent still held onto Shawn's hair, kept him in place. Shawn's pupils widened, his breath quickening.

"Yeah, sure."

"Are you going to bottom for me?"

"Oh Jesus, yes, Trent."

"Then let me suck you to sleep. That way we can be nice and rested so I can give you a good fuck later."

He watched as a play of different emotions danced across Shawn's face. He recognized the need, the desire—but there was something else. They stood that way for several seconds, completely silent, but never breaking their gaze. Finally, Trent moved in to take another kiss from Shawn then let him go.

They rinsed off, never far apart, always touching in one way or another. Trent reached behind Shawn to turn off the water, anxious to get them into his bed. Once they'd exited the shower and Trent had dried them both off, he was compelled to pick Shawn up again. He replaced the towels on the rack then faced Shawn, advancing toward him. Before he'd even had the chance to get in position to gather him in his arms, Shawn had grasped him around his neck. It no longer seemed to be an issue.

Once Trent held him, he nuzzled the top of his head, brushing his nose in the freshly cleaned damp waves. After lowering him onto the bed, Trent straddled him. Their heated erections were nestled against one another and Trent marveled that they'd been able to make it through the entire showering process without getting each other off, but he was enjoying the anticipation too much to rush it. He noted a slight tremble in Shawn's body.

"Cold?"

He shook his head. "Excited. Won't last long."

"Good. You need your rest."

Shawn drew his eyebrows together. "What about you?"

"I'll stroke myself off while I suck you."

"Like hell you will. I wanna make you come."

Trent leaned down to take his mouth again, not sure how he would ever get enough of Shawn's kisses. Yes. He wanted Shawn to make him come. Without breaking the contact of their lips, he dropped to one elbow then took Shawn's hand and placed it on his needy shaft. The moment Shawn wrapped his fingers around him, he almost shot his load. There'd been too much of a build-up. It had been fun, but he didn't want to wait anymore.

He growled into the kiss, pumping his dick into Shawn's fist. It had been so long since he'd been touched by anyone, since he'd wanted to be touched by anyone. His balls abruptly tightened, the surge of energy in his spine almost startling in its intensity.

"Oh, God, Shawn."

He froze, coming over and over on Shawn's hand, his stomach. He still rested on his elbows, but he dropped his forehead on Shawn's shoulder. He shuddered when Shawn released his softening member, every nerve alive right under the surface of his skin. His breathing gradually slowed and he lifted his head to gaze into Shawn's eyes.

"Beautiful."

He meant it in so many different ways and he was certain Shawn understood. Dipping his chin, he tasted Shawn's lips without deepening the kiss. He reached between them to rub his cum into Shawn's belly, stroked the soft hair of his happy trail. He was startled when Shawn pulled away to lick Trent's seed off his fingers.

"Jesus."

Trent had said it barely above a whisper. It was so hot between them, so immediate. Typically, Trent took a while to open up to someone. There were few with whom he'd ever even wished to do such a thing. It seemed as though once he'd decided to give Shawn a chance, he'd dropped every last bit of his resistance—caved in and allowed himself to feel everything.

Giving Shawn one more soft peck, he then lowered down the length of his body where he was met by Shawn's straining length. He'd been waiting all day for this one moment, the moment when he sucked Shawn, felt him on his tongue for the first time.

It was everything. Not so much that it was all he'd wanted it to be, but that it *was* everything. The soft skin encasing the heated erection. The sweet, full balls. His masculine scent highlighted by the clean soap smell. Shawn's strong thighs on either side of his head, tensing and bunching as he trembled under Trent's ministrations.

He swallowed Shawn down, allowed his mushroomed head to slide past his gag reflex—working the muscles of his throat until whimpers and cries fell from Shawn's lips, Shawn's heels digging in the mattress. He lifted off his dick with a strong suctioning pull, then teased his slit. Shawn grabbed his hair, his noises gaining in strength as he bucked his hips.

Trent increased his pace, the intensity. As Shawn thrust into his mouth, Trent shoved a hand under his ass to grab hold. He squeezed and kneaded his flesh even as he furiously ate Shawn's cock. Shawn's nuts drew tight right as he pulsed the first stream of hot cum into Trent's mouth. Immediately, there was a loud yell and Trent continued to milk Shawn's orgasm, pulling as much as he could from his lover.

As soon as Shawn went boneless on the bed, Trent let Shawn's softening member fall from his mouth and scooted up to gather him in his arms. He cradled Shawn, encouraging him to twine their limbs together. Soon, Shawn's breathing slowed and evened out. Trent smiled against the top of Shawn's head where it was tucked in the crook of his neck.

Yes. Sucked him to sleep.

Chapter Four

Floating. It didn't make sense because he was in the desert, surrounded by multi-colored rock vistas, scrub trees and cacti. It was so magnificent, more incredible than anything he'd ever seen. But he continued to float all around the spectacular sights. He wanted to take pictures, to capture the memories forever, but Trent was calling. And he wanted Trent more, because somehow he understood that Trent had given it all to him.

"It's almost six o'clock. I can throw a couple tuna steaks or some chicken on the grill if you'd like."

He was in Trent's arms. In his bed.

Fuck yeah.

"Hey."

One corner of Trent's lips curled up. "Did you hear me, sleepyhead?"

Shawn grunted, rubbing his eyes with one hand "Yes." He yawned. "Here, let me throw something on and I'll come help you."

He was already in motion, trying to roll away to launch himself from the bed, but Trent yanked him back.

"This first."

Before he knew what had happened, he was wrapped up in Trent's arms again, and Trent was pushing his tongue into Shawn's mouth. Shawn's dick hardened and his stomach rumbled simultaneously. Trent chuckled into the kiss, then let go.

"I know, me too."

Shawn wasn't sure if he'd meant that he was hungry or horny. But once Trent stood from the bed, he could see that horny was most certainly a big part of it.

Really big. Damn.

His own full erection was obviously of interest to Trent as well, since he openly stared at him. He wasn't particularly shy, but being around Trent gave him a sensation of vulnerability he'd never experienced before. Strangely, he liked it. He'd fought that feeling ever since his early days of being picked on by his brother and his brother's asshole friends. Being vulnerable in any way was not an option once he'd joined the force in Los Angeles. But it was different with Trent. It seemed right.

"Come on."

Trent had finally torn his eyes from him and jerked his head in the direction of the bathroom.

"I need a quick shower."

Chuckling Shawn remembered their recent encounter, running his hands across his stomach. It had been like Trent had marked him in his own way.

"I definitely need one."

Shawn glanced down in dismay at his dusty, dirty shorts. He'd brought an extra tee and some boxers, but hadn't thought to bring any jeans or anything else.

It was clear Trent had picked up on his quandary, as he'd headed to his dresser. He pulled a pair of black gym shorts from one of the top drawers.

"Here. These have a drawstring, so you can tighten them up if you need to."

Shawn snorted. "Oh, I'll need to."

"I'll go first."

He must have had a telling expression on his face, because Trent came over, grabbed his hand, and clamped his mouth on his for a quick, but claiming kiss. Once he let go, he looked intently into his eyes.

"We'll never make it to dinner otherwise."

Shawn admired the view as Trent ambled into the bathroom. He thought about at least ogling him while he washed up, but realized that what Trent had said about them becoming too distracted was probably true. Instead, he contented himself with reclining against the headboard of the bed. As he idly daydreamed, his mind wandered to the exquisite interlude they'd shared earlier. He surrendered to the fact that he was going to be hard no matter what he did.

After Trent exited the shower, he left the water running, calling out to him.

"Take your time. I'll get the grill started."

Shawn pushed himself up from the bed for his turn. Trent approached him, gloriously naked, semi-erect dick bobbing. Shawn tracked the droplets of water trailing down Trent's sculpted body, watching as they crossed the lines where the brown skin abruptly changed to white. Trent grabbed the back of his head, skimming his lips back and forth across Shawn's before finishing with a light peck.

"See you in the kitchen."

Trent patted his behind and left the room. The urge to rub out a quick one was achingly strong. He behaved himself, but washed in record time to stave off his weakening resolve. Since he didn't have his backpack in the bedroom to get his clean undies, he decided to free ball it. As he was pulling up the shorts, Trent entered, holding his pack.

"Uh, thanks."

He thought about dropping the shorts and putting on his underwear, but rejected it.

Oh well. Easier access later.

The thought had his dick springing back to life, which was way too obvious in his commando state. He didn't miss Trent's interest in his aroused condition.

"Food first. You'll want to be fortified for the evening."

The deep timbre of Trent's voice, the slight growl when he'd told him what they were going to do, had him right at the precipice of an orgasm once again. It was like a warm, welcoming mouth wrapped around his cock whenever Trent spoke to him like that. It was most definitely the only time in his life when he'd experienced such a thing.

They decided on the fish and while the grill warmed up, Trent put some brown rice in the cooker and Shawn sliced up some tomato and cucumber to go along with the salad. It was homey and comfortable, not at all how he'd pictured them being together for the first time. But it was good.

"Can you chop up these green onions too?"

"Sure. You want them in with the salad?"

"They're for the rice."

Shawn was curious, but he waited to see what sort of culinary magic Trent had in mind. Once they had everything ready, Trent took the steaks outside for a quick heating. By the time he was back inside, everything else was ready to go. He watched as Trent scooped up the rice and put it in a serving bowl. Then he added a couple of spoons of olive oil, some garlic salt and the onions Shawn had chopped up. He mixed it all together.

"Gives it some flavor."

Shawn nodded, his mouth watering. Not only did he and Trent have similar likes in food, but having a hunky, sexy man around who liked to cook? That was a recipe for endless wet dreams.

It had finally cooled down to a more bearable temperature of somewhere in the upper eighties, so they decided to eat out on the covered patio. It was blissfully relaxing and Shawn was so grateful that they'd managed to get together, and that the barriers Trent had put up had finally seemed to come down.

"You're thinking about something."

Shawn glanced up from the fork in his hand that had just been filled with a bite of the amazing rice. He chewed it then swallowed, wiping his mouth with one of the paper towels they'd brought outside.

"I'm glad things worked out so we could be together today—that you didn't run away from me like those times before."

Trent appeared uncomfortable, peering down at his plate and fiddling with his fork. Shawn had a twinge of regret for opening his big mouth. At the same time, as much as he liked it when other people spoke directly and didn't play games, he was the same way.

"I wasn't running." Trent frowned. "Maybe a little." He rubbed the back of his neck and glanced around before training his gaze on Shawn. "I think you can tell how much I like you. It just took me a bit to allow myself to take a chance again. That's all."

This time he didn't look away, but kept his eyes locked on Shawn.

"I get it." An unusual bout of shyness rose up in him. "Are you glad you took a chance?"

"Very."

Shawn's breath hitched a little. With one word Trent had conveyed a tremendous amount of intent. They went back to eating, silent for most of it. When they'd finished, Shawn rose to help Trent take in the dishes, but Trent laid a hand on his shoulder as he walked past.

"Stay here. I've got this."

He wanted to protest, but there was that tone in Trent's voice again that made him weak-kneed. Made him want to do whatever Trent asked of him. In a few minutes, Trent had reappeared with a bowl of assorted berries, topped with whipped cream. He had a flash of what they could do with those berries and cream, but figured that wasn't Trent's plan. At least, not immediately.

Trent peered up at him from a spoonful of fruit he'd just consumed, a dollop of the cream still clinging to his upper lip. He licked it up with a quick swipe of his tongue and Shawn groaned before he could stop himself. Trent gave him a quirky smile.

"You're quite the rascal."

Shawn snickered. "Rascal? Maybe." He cleared his throat. "So, I was curious 'cause I don't really know very much about you. I mean…were you born here in Vegas? Do you have family nearby?"

Trent arched his eyebrows then nodded. "I was going to ask you the same thing. Except for the Vegas part. I already know you're from LA."

"Vicki?"

"Nah. Lee told me."

Shawn shook his head. "Lee?"

"Best friend. We grew up together in Pahrump, and he's one of the guys at Station 32."

"Oh, *that* Lee. Is he…?"

"No. He's not gay. But we've known each other since kindergarten."

"Damn. I wish I had someone I'd been close to for that long." Shawn frowned. "How'd he know where I was from?"

Trent shrugged. "Usual inter-departmental gossip, I suppose." He locked eyes with Shawn again. "He informed me the day of the blood drive."

"Oh." Shawn squirmed in his chair. "Did you ask him?"

"Didn't have to. When you've known someone for as many years as we have, they can tell."

"Tell?"

"That I liked you."

Shawn swallowed, working up his courage. "I liked you then too."

"Hmmph."

"What?"

"I guess I was being silly."

Shawn reached across the small glass table and took Trent's hand.

"No you weren't. I understand now."

Trent squeezed his hand, but didn't let go. They talked some more, filling each other in on some highlights of their early years, why they'd chosen their respective careers. There had been similar reasons driving their job decisions. They both liked the outdoors, not being stuck behind a desk and the satisfaction of helping people.

Shawn also learned that Trent had been raised by a single mom that he didn't have much contact with—that they'd lived in a trailer and had barely scraped by. Shawn shared with Trent how his family, while big and middle class, didn't really want him around that much. Hadn't for a while. Their religious background didn't allow for a gay family member, unless, of course, he'd been willing to 'pray the gay away'.

The most revealing thing about their conversation was that they'd both been cursed with severely homophobic brothers.

"Chris told me he was glad I was moving away. He said that he was the only one in the family that had the courage to say to my face that he hated me—that they all felt that way about me."

"Fucking prick." Trent had a pained expression on his face. "I'm sorry."

Shawn exhaled slowly, the talk of his brother forming a knot in his stomach the way it always did. It was a reminder that he really was all alone in the world.

Trent stood then moved to kneel beside his chair. He took one of Shawn's hands and sandwiched it between his own.

"They obviously don't realize what they're missing by not having you in their lives."

Trent caressed him, his strokes strong and assured. Comforting.

A surprising wave of emotion rose up in him and for a disconcerting moment, he thought he might tear up. He swallowed around the lump in his throat to tamp it down. He needed Trent to take him away from the ugly thoughts their conversation had brought up.

"Take me to bed?"

Without answering, Trent rose then gently tugged on Shawn's hand, encouraging him to follow. The last thing Shawn needed was encouragement to go with Trent, but he liked the sensation of feeling wanted. Once they were inside his bedroom, Trent yanked Shawn to him, and any reserve they may have had left between each other was stripped away. They used their hands, lips and tongues frantically on one another. Even as they peeled off their minimal clothing, they remained in contact as much as possible.

Heavy breathing and urgent groans filled the air and Shawn remembered what Trent had asked him earlier—asked if he wanted to bottom for him. Even though he usually bottomed, the idea of Trent covering him with his strong, muscled body and driving into him with his generous length made him shudder. He whimpered.

The floor seemed to fall away and he realized he was in Trent's arms again. It was crazy how much he liked it. After all that had happened between them, he'd been sure that he would have fought being carried. After being tossed on the bed, Trent loomed over him, staring down at him.

"Gonna make you feel so good."

Trent moved fast, the mattress dipping as he pushed Shawn's legs open and back, exposing him to Trent's view. Shawn was rock-fucking hard and not sure how he could possibly last. He cried out as the moist heat of Trent's lips and tongue caressed his sac, laved his shaft then sucked briefly on his tip. Trent moaned, the vibrations going to his very core.

"Love your taste."

Trent had muttered it in between licks and sucks in an even raspier voice than normal. Never had he had a man love him with his mouth so thoroughly, so sensually. When Trent dipped to his hole, poking it with the end of his tongue, he startled, clenching his pucker. Trent ran one hand up his abdomen to his chest, pinching and tweaking his nipples. He used the other to hold Shawn in place, to hold him open as Trent greedily ate his ass.

"Please…" Shawn mewled.

His steeled erection bobbed against his belly as he writhed under Trent's oral attentions. Still Trent held him down, unable to do anything but take the pleasure he forced on him. Clutching the sheets in his fists, Shawn made a strangled animal noise, not sure where all his sounds were coming from. But he knew where all the sensations came from—Trent's touch, his mouth, his hold, the way he seemed to give everything over to making sure Shawn was taken care of.

Trent lifted his head then licked his way up from his hole, perineum, across his sac and up his length. He swirled around his helmeted head, pushing his tongue into Shawn's slit. Shawn reached for Trent, but Trent grabbed his wrists before locking his eyes on him. It was just before twilight—the room dim but not dark.

"I want in."

Shawn had his head lifted from the pillow and he nodded slightly before letting himself drop back down. His breathing was still accelerated from the overwhelming force of Trent's passion. He had never been so turned on to anyone before.

He'd been so lost in his own hazy thoughts that it wasn't until the cool trickles of lube ran down his crack that he was brought back to the present. He'd jumped a little in surprise and Trent whispered to him.

"I should've warmed that up with my hands first. I'll remember for next time."

Before he had a chance to ponder the 'next time' remark, he let out a sigh as Trent's finger sank into his channel. He clenched around it, wanting more but so grateful for what was already there.

"Oh, God, Trent. Wanted this."

"Mmm, yes. Me too. Gonna give you more."

Trent added a second digit and Shawn thrust, pushed against his hand, begging for it. Trent finger-fucked him nice and slow, digging deeper until he crooked his fingers to peg his gland. It wasn't merely good, it was mind shattering. He wanted to grab his own dick, but sensed that Trent wouldn't allow it. He knew his lover had a thing about being in charge. He couldn't temper a grin. Letting Trent be in charge of some things wasn't such a bad idea.

However, his nerves were alive—sparking and catching fire—and he needed something more. He grabbed a fistful of Trent's hair and held on.

"Stretch me. Fill me."

Trent leaned up and plunged into his mouth right as he added a third finger. He wanted to tell Trent that he couldn't keep control—that being invaded so forcefully at both ends was too much. But he loved it, wanted it. Trent worked him over good, did exactly as Shawn had begged. When he removed his hand and sat up, Shawn gave a low cry.

"Shh. Gonna get myself ready."

Watching Trent roll the condom over his gorgeous member then slick it up with more lube made him clench again. At last, he crawled between Shawn's legs, bringing one up so that it rested on his shoulder.

"Pillow?"

"S-sure."

At that point, he really didn't give a shit. All he cared about was being impaled by Trent's glorious cock. Trent shoved a pillow under Shawn's ass then the head of his gloved dick nudged against Shawn's hole. The leg that he didn't have over Trent's arm, he used to wrap around his waist, encouraging him on. Trent urged past his resisting ring of muscle and he hissed. Trent looked down on him with concern.

"More." He gritted out.

It had been a while, but he wasn't going to let that slow things down. He pushed out right as Trent thrust forward and within seconds, Trent was seated in his ass. They were connected, Trent's balls nestled against him, the slight bristle of his pubic hair tickling his skin.

"Don't move." Shawn whispered, his eyes closed.

"Are you okay?"

Shawn heard the worry in his voice yet he couldn't help but smile.

"More than okay. I just want to feel you like this for a minute."

He was so *full*. So filled with the most amazing man he'd ever met. He was aware of a slight throbbing inside his passage from Trent's needy cock. His own cock twitched. He could feel it leaking. His asshole clamped around the large member invading his body. He brushed his hands up Trent's torso, opening his eyes to look right at him.

"Fuck me."

Trent groaned in answer then pulled almost all the way out before slamming into him. He did his best to arch his back in the trapped position, tried with all he had to meet up with every snap of Trent's hips. The stretch, the burn, the everything wound him into a tightly coiled ball of need.

As their coupling increased in its frenzy, sweat gathered on his skin, and he felt small droplets fall on him from Trent. He opened his eyes again, mesmerized by how Trent's face twisted in an agonizing ecstasy as he fucked Shawn into oblivion. Suddenly, Trent's eyes went wide and as their gazes locked, it set them both off. Neither one of them looked away as they cried out in simultaneous release, their shouts echoing in the bedroom. Shawn had never seen anything so beautiful as Trent coming.

His insides milked Trent more, causing him to jerk in his passage. He rarely came without direct stimulation to his dick, but he'd been ready to shoot his load from almost the moment Trent had first tongued his hole. It would be so easy to get addicted to sex with him.

Trent eased Shawn's one leg down then slowly pulled out of him before removing the condom and disposing of it. He then stretched out and draped his body over Shawn's, holding himself up on his elbows so that Shawn wouldn't be crushed. Shawn couldn't deny how wonderful it was to be held down by Trent, to be underneath him, protected.

Wasn't that all he was trying to do before?

Trent took his mouth, lazily exploring it with his tongue. It was calming, brought him closer to his new lover, brought him down from his orgasmic high. It wasn't like so many of his previous encounters—even with men he'd had a relationship with—where they simply rolled off each other when the deed was done.

He *did* like feeling protected by Trent, wanted to be cherished by someone. But it couldn't be done from that place of fear Trent had shown him before. He was sure they were past that. Trent had to understand it couldn't be like that with them.

Trent broke the kiss but stayed close so that their breaths mingled.

"I have more berries—and more whipped cream."

Shawn raised his eyebrows. "Funny you should mention it. I'd had a dirty thought or two when you brought out the dessert earlier."

"I noticed. Let me get us a cloth to wash up with then I'll be right back. I plan on painting your entire body with that cream."

"That sounds cold."

"Maybe at first. But I'll make it hot."

Trent's eyes held a promise that Shawn was sure he would keep.

Chapter Five

Trent was back on shift at the fire station for the next couple of days and it was the first time in a while that he wished he wasn't there. It had been oddly difficult to drop Shawn off at his apartment that morning. Not that he'd thought he'd be anxious to see him go. It had more to do with how anxious he was that Shawn ever had to leave at all.

Taking a sip of the coffee he'd just poured as he stood in the station kitchen, Trent endeavored to work through everything in his mind. It wasn't easy—not when his emotions kept pushing rational thought out of the way and telling it to mind its own business. He was certain that what was happening was a good thing. That didn't stop it from being scary.

"Hey, there you are. You didn't call me back last night."

Right after their second helping of dessert and he'd licked Shawn clean, he'd heard the phone go off. Shawn had been dozing, so he'd disentangled himself to check that it wasn't something to do with work. He didn't typically leave a friend hanging like that, but he'd had an inexplicable urge to keep them both safely wrapped up in their own world for a while, to not let anything else intrude.

Lee stepped into the kitchen then grabbed the pot, pouring himself some coffee as well.

Trent was surprised to see him. "I didn't know you were in today."

"Took Ed's shift. His mom is in the hospital."

Trent winced. "Again. That's not good."

"I know, poor guy."

They both nodded then sipped at their drinks.

"So. Last night? I'd thought we could get together, maybe have a couple beers or whatever." Lee chuckled. "And I could hear the whole Walt and Shawn story. Man, he looked *pissed*."

He'll want details.

Trent frowned. "Walt or Shawn?"

Lee grunted. "Both, actually. But Walt made some snotty remarks to me before stomping off."

"I can imagine."

He took another swallow of the cooling liquid, keeping his eyes averted.

Lee scrutinized him. "What's going on?"

"Nothing."

"Bullshit. It's always hard to say for sure with you, Mr Stone Face, but you seem…satisfied. Or…happy?" Lee set his mug down then crossed his arms. "Or both." He inhaled and dropped his mouth open. "You got laid."

Trent whipped his head around. "Keep your voice down."

"You did!"

His shift had barely begun and already he was shaking his head. "Lee, we're not in high school."

"Please tell me it wasn't Walt."

"It wasn't Walt."

Lee stared at him expectantly then pursed his lips. "It wasn't Walt..." He made a gesture like he was expecting more.

"Right."

Trent took his coffee then sat at the dining table. Lee followed him, obviously not willing to admit defeat.

"Come on. I've wanted to see you get to this point for so long. Please tell me something good."

Lee had him there. A small twinge poked him in the gut. He knew how much Lee had suffered right along with him in his own way after Paul had died. If anyone deserved to know that he was feeling hopeful about things with Shawn, it was Lee. But it was no one else's goddamned business.

"Shawn and I spent the day together yesterday." He cleared his throat. "After I apologized about my whole restaurant fire behavior the day before, of course."

"Please tell me you spent the night together too?"

"Pervert."

Lee smacked him on the side of his arm.

"I don't need details, dickwad. Just tell me you like him and you think there's something there."

Trent snorted. "Definitely something there."

"And you're seeing each other again?"

Trent shook his head again. It was going to be one of *those* days.

"You in charge of my social calendar?"

"I'll take that as a yes."

Trent decided it was time to move Lee off the subject of his love life.

"Any follow-up on that fire at Showstoppers?"

"Oh shit, that's right. You haven't been here." Lee got a devilish grin on his face. "You were busy feeling up one of the local's finest in private instead of in public."

"Lee…" It had come out akin to a growl.

"Sorry. Turns out the Showstoppers fire was purposely set."

"Really?"

They had very few instances of arson in the city, particularly at any of the businesses on or near the Strip. There were too many people around the clock, cameras, security—even more so since 9/11. It was next to impossible to get away with anything like that. Although, since Showstoppers was a fairly new establishment, maybe they didn't have everything perfectly in place yet.

"Yeah. Even though the point of origin was in the kitchen, the investigative team found traces of an accelerant near the opening."

"Suspicious burn patterns?"

"Oh yeah, the usual. But what makes this one unusual was the anonymous letter sent to all the local media."

Trent pressed his lips together. All the city needed was some crazy running around. "What'd it say?"

"It's from a group. Citizens Against Immorality. It said they were on a mission to stamp out all deviant behavior from the City of Sin."

Trent smirked. "That's a rather broad statement, especially as the meaning of the word 'deviant' isn't the same for everyone. Any indicators as to who they are or that it really is a group and not some lone psycho."

"I heard from Darren that the investigative team thinks it's a group. They don't see how one person could pull off such a thing in a crowded restaurant without help."

Trent nodded. "I would tend to agree. It was packed in there that night."

Lee furrowed his brow. "And what in the name of all that is holy were you doing in a burlesque-themed restaurant?"

"Lee, really?"

"Just doesn't seem your thing."

"It's not."

The alarm sounded and they immediately jumped up to run and grab their gear. Trent switched into firefighter mode and endeavored to push aside any other considerations. The next free moment he had, he would text Shawn. Since he wasn't much of a talker, phones weren't his best friend but texting worked. A few choice words would be nice so he could have that connection with Shawn that he already missed—already wanted all the time.

* * * *

He couldn't stop grinning. Truthfully, he was sure he looked like an idiot. From the occasional odd glances Vicki gave him, he figured she probably thought so too. He turned his attention to the alcohol-fueled madness all around them. Even though it was a Tuesday night, people were still out in droves. He and his partner remained as vigilant as ever.

"Ever planning on telling me how it went?" She smirked. "Although I think I can guess."

His happy grin instantly morphed into a scowl. "How did you…?"

"The man grilled me like a cheese sandwich when I first got to the station the other day. After I gave him some advice—and info—I told him you'd texted me that you were on your way. That's how."

"I never said I forgave him—or anything."

"No. But the goofy smile you've had on your face all night told on you."

Shawn couldn't make eye contact. Even though it was doubtful the flush he felt crawling up his neck would be visible amidst the garish nighttime lights of the Strip, he didn't want her to read the expression in his eyes—the one that would give everything away when he thought about Trent.

Still mindful to keep his gaze averted, he really wanted to at least let her know that things seemed like they might work out between him and Trent. He'd never been super social and the few guys he'd hung out with back in California hadn't been close friends—more like buddies to chill with. Now that he wasn't there to go grab a beer or movie with, he was of little interest.

He supposed it was mutual. It wasn't that he didn't want to be close to anyone. He did. It was more that he tended to focus on fewer people. Quality over quantity. His family had certainly taught him that lesson. When he did get into a relationship, he concentrated his energy on that person. It worked for some and not for others. He hoped it was something that would work for Trent.

"Okay, Ruiz. We went out the other day. And yeah, it was good." He smiled to himself again. "Real good."

"Enough. I don't need to know any more."

"Don't worry. That was all you were gonna get."

She fixed her gaze on him.

"You sure about that? You seem awfully starry-eyed over there."

He gave her a look of irritation and she chuckled.

"You're an easy target, Everly."

"Funny."

A woman screamed and their attention was drawn to an area between a chain motel and a liquor store. Off in the darkness near some bushes, a woman struggled with someone. Shawn lunged forward, drawing his Glock 17. Vicki radioed in for backup as she followed him. If they were lucky, Darren and Parker would be close by.

"Las Vegas Police! Show us your hands!"

The attacker threw the woman to the ground and Vicki ran to her aid. He took off running and Shawn gave chase. Almost immediately, Darren and Parker pulled into the motel lot and Shawn gestured frantically in the direction of the suspect. Darren joined in the foot pursuit while Parker pulled into the alleyway behind the motel, no doubt hoping to cut the guy off.

It worked perfectly. The attacker hadn't expected the cruiser and ran into the immobile vehicle so hard, he bounced off it before he hit the ground. Parker leaped out of the car and pounced on him. Darren joined his partner in collaring the guy, but he'd already given up the fight. After verifying that Darren and Parker had things under control, he headed back to where Vicki and the woman were near the front. He jogged through the motel parking lot then hit the ground knee first. Landing with a thump, he managed to tear a sizeable hole in his pants. Blood trickled from his knee and he thought he might have even sprained it. He looked around for the source of his tumble and noted a tree root pushing up from the asphalt near the edge of the motel office.

Son of a bitch.

He felt like a walking disaster film. The department was going to think he was jinxed. He heard sirens approaching and assumed that Fire and Rescue had been called out to help the woman. Right then, Parker and Darren rolled by. They stopped and Darren hopped from the vehicle.

"What the hell happened?"

So fucking embarrassing.

"I, uh… I guess I tripped."

Fortunately, Darren and Parker had always been cool. But that didn't mean that he might not be the recipient of some good-natured ribbing. Hell, if things were reversed, he probably would do the same thing.

"Isn't Vicki supposed to be keeping an eye on you? Technically, you're still the new guy. I think we're gonna have to have a talk with her."

"Very funny. Can you help me up?"

"That's a negative."

"Huh?"

Was he going to be a dick after all?

"You're not moving until paramedics get here."

Shawn groaned. "Oh come on. I banged my knee up a little, it's no big deal."

"That's their call, not mine. Stay put."

Already a crowd had gathered. First it had been the woman and now he was on display as the evening's entertainment. It really had to stop. Darren waved Vicki over.

"Everly, I can't leave you unattended for five minutes."

"Not in the mood, Vicki."

Darren turned to her. "I'm disappointed in you, Ruiz. But maybe you can make it up to him by holding his hand until the medics get here."

Darren had said it with such seriousness that it almost made him want to laugh, even if he was the main recipient of the mockery.

"Sorry. I've gotta wrap things up with the victim over there."

"Hey, Vicki, she all right?"

"Yeah. It's a domestic, but they're not even gonna transport her. Someone is coming down to give her a ride."

"Thank God for that."

He heard more sirens.

Oh shit. Trent's on tonight.

Darren glanced down at him. "Sounds like your ride's almost here. Trent's not gonna beat me up for letting something bad happen to his boyfriend, is he?"

Shawn couldn't stop his jaw from dropping. He whipped his head around to glare at Vicki.

She put her hands up. "I never said anything. I didn't even know for sure until tonight."

"What do you mean 'for sure'. No one knew anything at all."

Darren sputtered out laughter. "Right. Everyone knew it was only a matter of time—especially the way he's had his paws all over you this past week. Never mind the meaningful, Twilight-worthy stares you've both been sharing with each other."

Shawn was pissed. The fuck. Off. It must have showed.

"Hey, hey, Shawn. Don't be mad. We're actually really glad for you guys." He squatted down next to him, bringing his voice down. "Look, a lot of us knew Paul. liked him a lot. It was hard on everyone when we lost him, but watching Trent go through that was devastating. He's always been such a tough guy, no visible emotions. After Paul died, it was excruciating to see him work so hard to remain stoic every day. Sometimes I wanted to shake him and tell him to let it all out." He patted Shawn's arm. "You have no idea how nice it is to see him get soft about someone. And I mean that in the best possible way."

Shawn wasn't able to formulate actual words. He'd never really thought about what the other officers must have been through as a result of Paul's murder. Of course they would have known him, had a relationship with him. He'd only been focused on Trent's personal relationship with his lover.

The lights on the Fire and Rescue truck approaching blinded him, kept him from seeing where it was from right away. Two guys jumped down and ambled over to him. He was finally able to adjust his eyes and read the side. They were from Station 11. Maybe 32 was on another call. It was hard to say. He pondered whether to phone Trent. If he was at an incident or asleep at the station, he wouldn't want to be interrupted. On the other hand, he didn't want to have him find out through someone else. It had become startlingly clear that everyone blabbed to everyone else across all the departments. Maybe that was the case for all work scenarios, but it was just that he was the one who was blab-worthy for the first time ever.

After an examination by the medics, they were sure it was only a sprain, but they insisted on transporting him so he could be checked out at the hospital. An ambulance arrived to cart him off and he noted that his little tumble had kept a group of bystanders interested right up until he was loaded into the back of the truck. It was amusing from the standpoint of there being so many other things much more interesting going on in the immediate vicinity. But he supposed it was all relative. Those people probably saw a lot of the same shit every night. At least a police officer tripping was different.

It was well past midnight by the time he got to the hospital, so he decided he'd wait and send Trent a text in the morning. He'd be getting off his shift at noon anyway, so it would be better that he not have anything bothering him before then.

No hiking this weekend, dammit. Or foot patrol.

He was sure they'd find other things to keep themselves busy—he grinned at that thought. But he'd been looking forward to the drive they'd planned for the day they both had time off. Still, it was nice to have that comfortable feeling where he knew that it was okay if they didn't get to that drive right away. Somehow he knew they'd have plenty of other opportunities in the future.

* * * *

Trent washed off in one of the shower stalls in the station. Only a few more hours to go before he was off shift. After he made some breakfast, he'd send Shawn a text. Maybe they could grab some lunch before Shawn went to work. It'd be difficult to get together too much before their planned excursion to Spring Mountain at the weekend, but he hoped they could at least grab a few hours here and there.

After toweling off and getting dressed, he ambled out to the kitchen. Most of the guys ate whatever they could find laying about, some of them eating sandwiches around the clock unless someone else cooked. Trent almost always made something fresh. If he didn't have time, he would at least make a high protein drink. When both he and Lee pulled a shift together, his friend made sure to sniff around the kitchen as much as possible—just in case.

He scrambled some eggs and heated a few slices of lean ham. Sure enough, Lee showed up by his side, seemingly from out of nowhere.

"Mmm. What's for breakfast?"

First words he'd heard all morning and already he was shaking his head.

"Eggs and ham. Where're the other guys?"

"Zonked out. Damn, it was busy last night. If things stay quiet, I might grab a nap later."

"Even the captain?"

"Guess so. The office was dark."

Trent nodded, pushing at the eggs with the spatula. Once he'd made two plates, he handed one to Lee then took his to the table. They ate in silence for a while. Jamal shuffled into the room, yawning and stretching.

"How'm I supposed to sleep with that tasty aroma of food wafting through the station?"

Trent grunted, but continued eating.

"Not only that, but your cell buzzed a couple times. You must've forgot to put it on silent."

He didn't want to appear obvious—or excited. The only person who could possibly be trying to reach him would be Shawn. Other than Lee, he didn't have many people he socialized with or who would be calling so early. He quickly finished up, pointedly ignoring the amused stares from Lee. Rising to wash off his plate and utensils as quick as he could, he froze when Lee grabbed his arm.

"I got it."

"Why?" he was thoroughly confused.

Lee arched his eyebrows and gave him a look as though Trent was the dumbest man alive.

"I said, I *got* it. You made breakfast, so it's only fair."

Jamal snorted. "That's a good one. Since when?" He continued shoveling food into his mouth from where he stood, leaning against the counter.

Lee rolled his eyes and bobbed his head in the direction of their shared bedroom.

"Thanks."

He couldn't deny that he was grateful to Lee but wondered at his own behavior. It was bewildering to him that his heart could leap with joy, flutter in his chest at the mere thought of Shawn contacting him. Things seemed right, *felt* right. Seemed like they were clicking on all levels as a couple. But it was new and he hoped it all wasn't only because he was desperate to have someone in his life again.

Once he reached the room, he snatched up his phone and tapped the 'messages' icon. It was from Shawn and his heart went from fluttering to clenching in record time.

Everything's ok, but banged up my knee last night. Won't be on shift til next Monday. No hiking either. ☹ But wouldn't mind some company.

He skipped the texting and went straight to phoning. His hand shook and he wanted to kick himself. If he came across too upset—too over-protective—he could piss Shawn off. They were doing really well and he didn't want to derail anything.

Will I be able to handle caring so much?

A stray thought that he might be suffering from PTSD wandered through his mind, then Shawn picked up.

"What happened?" He winced at his own frantic tone.

"You got my text. Obviously." Shawn sounded cranky.

Clearing his throat, he tempered his voice. "I apologize. I..." He...what?

"I know."

There was a silence and it was Trent's gut that clenched instead of his heart. He heard a sigh on the other end of the line.

"Let's start over. I'm glad you called. It's good to hear from you."

Trent took a deep breath. "I'm glad I called too. I...I miss you." He searched around for something to say that didn't involve grilling Shawn on what had happened. He had nothing.

"I tripped."

Trent was thrown off by the statement. Then he realized Shawn was referring to his knee injury. In which case, Trent felt like a real dope.

"I see. You said everything's okay, but no walking for a while?"

The moment Shawn chuckled, all the tension left Trent's body. It was unbelievable the marked difference between the two states of being. Maybe he should've met with a counselor after losing Paul, the way Lee had hounded him to.

"It was so humiliating. I'd chased after a suspect, no problem, then jogging back to where Vicki was I tripped over a damn tree root in the parking lot of a motel. Talk about stupid."

"It's not stupid. Pulled muscle?"

"Sprain. Contusion on the kneecap. I'm supposed to go back to work on Monday if the doctor clears me."

"Okay then." He searched around in his brain to find a way to delicately bring up the next part. "I'm coming to get you when I'm off work. You're staying at my house this week."

He wasn't good at delicate—or subtle.

"I am? You're not much of an asker, are you?"

"Were you going to say no?"

He heard Shawn groan. "I suppose not. But I don't want to be a hassle or be in your way."

"I never would have asked—I mean, told you—if I didn't want you there."

"I guess I've figured that out about you. Which I do like, by the way."

"Good. I'll be there in a few hours. Don't move around getting ready, I'll help you pack up when I get there."

"Am I being told again?"

"Yes."

Shawn snorted. "Okay then."

Chapter Six

He was simultaneously irritated and thrilled that Trent had demanded he stay with him for the week. Ever since they'd talked, he had worked the conversation through his mind, trying to discern what it was that had him pulled in two different directions. Sure, he was madly in lust with Trent, thought there could be more—but he wasn't a child, or helpless. He'd spent most of his life sucking it up and handling everything on his own with little or no outside support. He hardly needed another human being to be there for him all the time.

He became surprisingly emotional. Picking at the blanket covering his legs, he bit at his bottom lip to keep from crying like a big baby. Of course he'd handled things on his own. No one had cared enough in forever to show him any support, any consideration. Once his family knew about him, it had all gone away and been replaced by disgust. Hatred.

Everything swirled around in his gut as he realized he absolutely adored the way Trent took charge of him, how he nakedly showed his concern. Was that the only reason he had such an immediate closeness to him? Yet, they had an undeniable attraction, one that had occurred way before Trent had been his hero at the Bellagio. They also had a lot in common, so there was that too. If he added all of that along with how good he felt when he was with him—that had to outweigh anything else.

Didn't it?

"Fuck."

His excitement at being with Trent for the week was getting messed with and it pissed him off. He wanted to smack himself upside his head at all of his overthinking, although he managed to save a healthy portion of his anger for his family. Any weird issues he had plaguing him over beginning a relationship with Trent was their doing.

But letting it continue is my doing.

He took a deep breath. That was it then. He'd wanted to get with Trent from the moment he saw him. It was that simple. It had never been about wanting someone to take care of him. If Trent answered a need in him that was in addition to all the other things he liked about the guy, then so be it.

Like a lot.

Of course, he still didn't want Trent freaking out every time he got a paper cut. He snickered to himself. It *was* kind of cute how Trent melted around him, turned into a fuzzy teddy bear worrying over him. A warm squishy feeling gathered low in his belly. He was guilty of some melting too.

The buzzer sounded and he lifted the blanket then removed the ice pack he'd had on his knee. He laid it on the glass coffee table. Grimacing as he pushed himself up from the couch, he limped over to the intercom, making sure he spoke into it before letting Trent in.

"Trent?"

"Yeah. Thanks for that."

He chuckled. It was a start to a comfortable compromise. He unlocked the door then hobbled back to the couch. He'd no doubt never hear the end of it if he was standing when Trent came in.

Shit. The crutches.

He jumped up too fast and gritted his teeth in pain. His whole 'sitting down like a good boy' plan would be shot to hell if he didn't have the crutches next to him instead of propped by the front door. Grabbing them, he made it back to the couch—only mildly out of breath—before he heard Trent's knock.

"It's open."

Trent entered the room, the look of disapproval on his face mild in comparison to the usual one.

"I asked before I buzzed, remember?"

Trent had the decency to look contrite.

"Of course."

Shawn waited for what he was sure would be an extended interrogation, but instead Trent immediately came to him on the couch. He wrapped him in a heartfelt hug then sought out his lips. Shawn gladly opened up to him, instantly taken back to that place where he never wanted to be anywhere else but in Trent's arms. His kisses were astounding in their sweetness. It had actually surprised him that such a masculine, hunky guy like Trent was so into kissing. Somehow it seemed out of character. But after experiencing their intensity, he wouldn't want it any other way.

"Can I see?"

They released one another, yet remained close.

"It's not that exciting. The bruise is pretty harsh looking. There's a scrape too, fucked up my pants."

Trent examined it, frowning. "Aren't you supposed to have this wrapped?"

"I was icing it before you got here. Plus, I have to change the bandage on the scrape."

"I'll help."

"Trent..."

"I'm here. I'll help."

He'd decided it was okay to want to have someone care for him now and then and since Trent seemed to want to do it, what the hell.

Shawn already had everything out, but Trent insisted he have another fifteen minutes with the ice before they took off. He said it would give him time to get Shawn's things packed up. There was a brief argument when Shawn insisted on directing him on what he needed by following him into the bedroom. Most of it revolved around whether Shawn would use the crutches or be carried. The crutches won the first round.

"Briefs in the top drawer on the left. Socks on the right. Any of the tees in the drawer below are fine."

Trent had been efficiently opening and closing drawers, grabbing items as he went and stuffing them into a large overnight tote.

"Sweats and shorts would be the easiest with the wrap—those are on the bottom." He thought of something and his eyes widened in horror. "Wait!"

It was obviously too late. He covered his face. The heat in his skin was so strong it warmed the palm of his hand. He refused to look.

"Shawn? You bringing this?"

He parted his fingers to see Trent holding up his dildo. His rather large dildo. It hadn't seen any action in a while, so he'd forgotten about it. Dropping his hand in resignation, he sighed.

"You asked. Wow. That's a first."

"In that case…"

Trent dropped it in the bag. He shot up his eyebrows. That wasn't what he'd expected Trent to do. Learning about someone new was all kinds of fun. Trent reached back in the drawer and pulled out a couple of his porn DVDs.

"I'll leave these behind. You'll be taken care of."

Perfect. He was hard.

Trent lifted the corner of his mouth in a smirk. "We should get you out of here. Might be a good idea to get you in my bed as soon as possible." Trent's expression became serious. "Maybe not."

"Are you kidding? That's evil."

Walking over, Trent then stood next to him where he reclined on the bed, his leg propped up. Trent carded his fingers through his hair.

"I'm worried about your knee."

"We'll wrap the shit out of it and avoid doggy style."

He could practically see the wheels turning in Trent's head. "I could ride you."

"You… Where did that come from? Not that…you know…I'm against it."

Trent grunted. "You could lie on your back, not have to bend your knee."

The man had a point. However, he was also adding to his arousal agony.

"Yeah, good plan. Can we go now?"

Leaning over, Trent planted a firm kiss on his lips.

"Let me get the rest of your things."

There was a nice quirk at the corners of Trent's mouth as he rose and gazed into his eyes. His questioning thoughts from earlier were erased by what he saw in those eyes. There was no doubt in his mind that there was a true connection between them. Where it would take them, he wasn't completely sure, but he was hopeful. Really hopeful.

* * * *

Trent had tolerated the crutches from Shawn's apartment to the truck. Then he'd allowed it up his walkway and in the front door. The minute they were inside his home however, he was done. He'd scooped up a not-so-surprised Shawn and carried him to the bedroom. Truthfully, he thought he'd done rather well so far. He'd only fussed over him a little.

He got Shawn settled in bed then eyed the duffle. When he'd spied the dildo in the bottom of Shawn's drawer, he'd had to ignore his first instinct which had been to grab his own dick. He'd never used any sex toys before, but the thought of the phallus shoved up Shawn's ass had tightened his balls instantly, had him leaking in his jeans. How he'd made it out of there without ripping Shawn's clothes off was a miracle.

"Hey, I didn't want you to go to any trouble."

Trent continued grabbing handfuls of the old shirts he used to work out in from a drawer and laid them on top of the dresser.

"This is hardly trouble. Don't worry about it."

After he'd finished clearing the space, he unzipped Shawn's overnight tote. He heard a groan and glanced over his shoulder.

"Are you in pain? Let me get your pain meds out." He dug around in the bag.

"No, that's not it. I took one before you arrived."

Trent turned around. "What's wrong?"

"The only pain I'm in right now involves my mortification caused by a certain item you discovered in my bedroom. I'm sure you were about to remove it from my duffle."

He couldn't help but grin—something he wasn't widely known for. "Only way I can use it on you is if I remove it."

Shawn grabbed his crotch and winced. "Jesus, Trent. That was really hot."

"Anyone ever done that before?"

"Said something hot to me?"

He smirked. "Used the toy on you. Or did you only use it on yourself?"

Biting his lower lip, Trent watched as Shawn rubbed his dick through the loose fabric of his sweats.

"Too much Trent, your voice, talking like that. Fuck, you'll make me come."

He considered Shawn's words. They gave him an idea for the future when they might have trouble seeing one another. But it would also be a good way to get Shawn off where he had the control, since his injury was so recent.

"Answer me."

"Oh, Jesus. On myself, no one else."

"Good. From now on, you only use it on yourself when I'm watching."

A small whimpering sound came from Shawn. He moved his hand more insistently along his length.

"Take it out."

Trent leaned comfortably against the large piece of bedroom furniture, his arms crossed in front of him. He watched in satisfaction at the shocked expression on Shawn's face. It seemed clear that he'd never experienced anything like what they were doing. In truth, neither had Trent.

"Um…"

"Take it out. You know where the lube is."

"Are you gonna…?"

"Not today. You're going to stroke yourself while I watch."

Shawn nodded shakily. After he'd twisted his body to reach the nightstand drawer, he retrieved the tube then pulled his erection over the top of the sweat pants. The head was nice and dark red, the moisture beading at the end obvious. Trent was transfixed at the sight. He instinctively moved his hand to his own dick and rubbed.

"That's it. Slick it up real nice for me. Stroke it good. Show me how you like it."

"Uhnh, fuck me."

"Later. Tell me more about the dildo. Do you lie on your back and spread your legs for it? I bet you finger yourself real good first. How many do you use?"

Shawn had established a rhythm on his cock, occasionally using his thumb to press in the slit as he passed over the head. His breathing was erratic, his hips pumping gently into his fist. Trent couldn't stand it any longer. He unzipped his pants before grabbing his own heated shaft, pausing only to lick his palm.

"Start off with two." Shawn gasped, arching his back somewhat. "Work up to four."

"Do you go deep? Or just inside your hole with short stabbing thrusts?"

"Trent, oh God, Trent." Shawn moved languidly, angled to one side, seemingly careful to keep his hurt knee still. "Both." He inhaled deeply. "Depends on my mood."

"Now the toy. Describe putting it in your ass."

"I'm gonna shoot."

"Not yet. Dildo first. Imagine you're alone, you don't want to come yet, you want it to last."

"This is so..." He licked his lips. "Uh... I part my legs, bend and lift them. Oh..."

Shawn hissed and Trent watched as he suddenly stilled then pressed a finger against the base of his cock. His head fell back and he panted almost out of control. Trent knew how he felt. He slowed his own jacking or he'd have to stop his climax too. As soon as Shawn's breathing slowed, Trent spoke again.

"Do you reach between your legs or around the back to insert it?"

"I... I reach around." Shawn slowly picked up a rhythm on his dick again. "Easier."

"Then?" Trent increased the pace on his own throbbing erection.

"I play...play a little. Tease my hole..." Shawn's eyes were closed, his face flushed. "Poke it in and out, just past the rim...oh...fuck."

"Feels good, doesn't it? Your tight little pucker getting stretched over and over, the hard toy invading your insides. Tell me what happens when you ram it all the way up your ass."

Ropes of cum shot from Shawn's cock as he let out a garbled cry. It was all Trent needed to come profusely over his own hand, his moans added to Shawn's sounds. He milked the last bit of spunk from his softening member, breathless, thoroughly sated. Shawn was collapsed on the bed as if he'd passed out and Trent felt a strong sense of satisfaction. He'd done that—made Shawn come unreservedly without even touching him. As a side benefit, he'd also received wonderful instructions on how he could use the toy on Shawn another time so that it really pleased him.

He went to the washroom to grab a couple of cloths that he moistened with warm water, then brought them to the bed to clean them both up. Sitting down, he noted the play of a smile on Shawn's lips. Even if they hadn't touched during their mutual masturbation, he still wanted a kiss. Wanted to connect them physically in the afterglow.

He leaned down then took what he wanted, licking inside his mouth as Shawn easily parted for him. He alternated between sucking in a lip then dipping in for more, tasting what he knew he would never get enough of. Straightening, he brushed Shawn's hair back from his forehead.

"Rest. You said you sometimes liked comfort food. Tell me."

Shawn opened his eyes that were still glazed from his release. "Might sound funny, but Chinese. I don't normally eat fried food, but once in a while… You know?"

"I do. There's a place nearby that delivers."

The smile on Shawn's face increased. "Can't bear to leave my side."

Trent locked eyes with his.

"No. I can't."

* * * *

Shawn had been at Trent's house for a few days and he had to admit he was glad the guy had insisted. Not that he'd really *had* to insist, but if nothing else, he was thrilled he hadn't been given a choice.

I've lost it.

It was obvious he was in trouble when it came to Trent. Even though it had never been clearly stated, there was no doubt that what he and Trent were doing was exclusive. They were together. Once he'd let go of his earlier hesitation about being with Trent, he'd embraced everything that had happened so far between them. In a very short time he'd become attached.

With Trent being gone on shift for two days at a time, there weren't any fears about needing his space. And since it was so new between them, it was the exact opposite. He honestly wished Trent was there every minute. The way Trent remained at his side constantly confirmed that his lover was experiencing the same feeling.

His knee was doing better and he'd gotten past the three-day-no-walking rule. He was still supposed to go easy and keep it wrapped, but he didn't have to rely on the crutches all the time. He'd kept his leg propped up on the couch all morning, using heat instead of ice. Since Trent would be home soon and off for the next couple of days, he planned to be in as good a shape as possible. The man still owed him a ride.

He pressed his palm against his gym shorts. His dick strained against the briefs, ready for whatever action it could get. It was difficult not to think of it as a separate entity—he'd had no control over it since he'd been with Trent. As if on cue, his man unlocked the door, a smile on his face as he walked in. Shawn noticed that lately he'd come across lighter, happier than he recalled from when he first knew him.

"How're you doing?"

"Excellent. Especially now."

Trent set his bag down then sauntered toward him. Shawn swung his knee off the couch to make room. He wanted Trent next to him.

"Keep your leg up."

"No."

They both paused, each of them seemingly surprised by Shawn's declaration.

"I've had my leg up almost the entire time you've been gone. I'm supposed to be walking on it now and then at this point. I want you next to me. I missed you."

Trent appeared to mull his words over then nodded. "Okay."

Shawn almost sighed in relief. He hadn't really believed that he had no voice in his relationship with Trent, but it was nice to know he could put his foot down once in a while. Literally, under the circumstances. He snorted.

Trent sat right next to him so their bodies touched then angled his head to take a kiss. It started out chaste but quickly caught fire. Trent clasped his hand, squeezing it before he let go of his mouth. Shawn exhaled at the loss. They remained close, nuzzling one another.

"Missed you too."

"Liked your texts."

Trent chuckled. "I bet you did."

"Were you able to get anything out of them too?"

"Almost."

Barely suppressing a laugh, Shawn nipped at Trent's chin before speaking.

"Almost?"

"Had to yank a blanket over me when Lee burst in the room."

"Oh shit. When was that?"

"Last night, after dinner."

"Was that when…?"

Trent nodded. "You wrote you had your tongue in my hole."

"Oh, baby, I'm so sorry." The laughter bubbled up before he could stop it. "I thought you didn't get back to me right away because you'd come and had to go clean up or something."

"That would have been the reason."

"It could be a reason later."

"You want your tongue in me?"

"Ride my face then ride my pole."

Trent groaned. "You are such a rascal."

"You don't want to feel me in you?"

Grabbing him to his body, Trent suckled the lobe of his ear as he hugged him tight.

"I never wanted anything more. But I'm gonna feed you first."

"Are we still talking dirty or did you actually mean lunch?"

Pulling back, Trent cradled his face with his hands.

"Lunch. I'll need my strength to ride that thick pole."

"You hardly ever talked before and now everything that comes out of your mouth is filthy. I love it."

"I only talk like this for you."

"Damn straight."

They both relaxed against the couch cushions, Trent with his arm resting behind Shawn, Shawn's hand on Trent's knee.

"What're you in the mood for?"

Shawn arched his eyebrows and Trent had obviously caught his expression.

"Food wise."

"Well, I boiled some eggs last night and there's some turkey and cheese in the fridge still. I could throw together a makeshift Cobb salad."

"I'll do it. You might be getting better, but you're still not a hundred percent. Plus, you boiled the eggs."

"Yeah, that required great effort."

"Smart ass. I can make some garlic toast to go with it."

"You know, it's a damn good thing we both like garlic."

Trent gave him a smirk. "No kidding."

Shawn made his way into the kitchen area, sitting at the table to keep Trent company while he put their meal together.

"Did you see the coverage on the news about the latest arson attempt?"

"Yeah, craziness. I called Vicki to see if she knew anything that hadn't been reported."

"And?"

"Not much more than what's already out there. I guess they're keeping the investigation real quiet."

Trent chopped tomatoes while he talked. "The captain hinted we'd be getting some sort of briefing real soon. I don't like not knowing what we're up against—what to be on the lookout for. I don't know why they're being so cagey about this."

Shawn considered what Trent had said.

"You think it's some sort of terrorist thing?"

"No, I think it's some sort of group of barely functioning nutjobs kind of thing, especially after their latest failed attempt to light up some of the big hotels."

For the past couple of days there had been repeated small fires lit in various resort casinos, some occurring simultaneously. That alone had put to rest the conjectures over whether or not the acts were being committed by a lone person. Fortunately, none of the small blazes had amounted to much, some doing no more than smoking before being put out.

Successfully doing any real damage to the world-class resorts bordered on the laughable. After the deadly MGM Grand and Hilton fires in the early eighties, there hadn't been one hotel fire death or significant incident of fire. Strict codes and safety measures had turned the Strip into one of the safest places to visit in the United States.

They moved off the topic of arson and onto discussing the next couple of days they had available to spend together as they dug into their food. After taking a few bites of salad, Trent set his fork down.

"I was thinking, just because you can't hike doesn't mean we can't take a drive out to Spring Mountain, stop for lunch somewhere. I'm sure there're some viewpoints where we could pull over if you want to take some pictures."

"Sounds awesome. The cabin fever is setting in. I'm used to a lot more activity."

He watched as a hint of playfulness flickered in Trent's eyes. "After we finish up here, I can help you out with some activity."

"Oh really? I hope we're picking up where we left off earlier."

"We are. I hope you're ready for the ride of your life."

Chapter Seven

Trent adjusted the temperature in the Jacuzzi. He was anxious, needy. It had been a long time since he'd bottomed for anyone, even if he knew he'd be a bit toppy with Shawn. Although he loved having his ass fingered, licked—he didn't love being fucked. He'd suggested partly out of worry over Shawn's condition plus the desire to experience everything he could with him.

After lunch they'd been too desperate for one another to get creative. His original plan of climbing on top of Shawn had been derailed as soon they'd both been naked. Grinding against each other on the mattress until their pre-cum slicked cocks slid together in an urgent dance, they'd come before they'd gotten any further. They'd napped then watched a movie in bed before making dinner.

As he set the scene out on his private patio, he waited for Shawn, who was busy pouring them some spiked lemonade. He'd apparently been bored enough while Trent had been at the fire station that he'd made some fresh. Since Shawn had stopped taking the painkillers, Trent had busted out the small bottle of vodka he had in one of the kitchen cabinets.

He reclined on one of the patio loungers. Even though his yard was shielded from the neighbors by high cement block walls and hedges, he'd turned off the outdoor lights. The only illumination was from a few small votive candles he'd set around. Towels, lube and a condom were close by. The music of the band Elbow played softly—he'd directed the speakers from his iPod bay toward the outdoors.

It had been his idea to use the Jacuzzi—it would be soothing to Shawn's knee. And it was sexy, romantic even. Not that he knew or thought all that much about such things, but Shawn had seemed to motivate him in ways he'd never believed anyone could.

"Holy shit. The sexiest man alive is lying out here. Must be my lucky night."

Shawn emerged from the living room, the two iced drinks in his hands. Trent took the one that Shawn offered him, unsuccessfully controlling his frown. There was no wrap on Shawn's leg and he still had a noticeable limp. Shawn must have caught his expression.

"I'm fine." He sat in one of the patio chairs. "You're going to do all the work anyway, right?" Shawn chuckled before taking a sip of the lemonade.

Trent took a drink too. It was refreshing, tart with a kick of warmth as it went down.

"That I will. All you need to do is relax."

Shawn held his gaze as he drank again. He placed the glass on the small outdoor table.

"Except for my tongue. I plan on giving that a thorough workout."

He hadn't been so hard, so much, since he could remember. There was something about Shawn that spoke to him on a completely primal level. He took a generous swallow of the lemonade then set it down. Just as if he hadn't come earlier in the day and all the days before, he was ready for more with his lover.

As he stood, he extended his hand, dropping the towel he'd had wrapped around his waist. "Come on."

Shawn accepted it, allowing him to not only lead him but to remove his shorts before helping him into the tub.

Sighing, Shawn closed his eyes as he sank into the water. "Fucking fantastic idea."

Trent climbed in and floated over to where Shawn reclined against the side. Straddling him, he allowed himself to enjoy the buoyancy, the bubbles. The peacefulness. He braced himself with one hand on the ledge and used the other to caress Shawn's torso. It was impossible to imagine anything more enjoyable than touching his body, tasting it, plundering it. He played in the light dusting of hair across Shawn's chest, pinching and teasing each nipple until they plumped up.

"God, Trent. What you do to me."

Shawn still had his eyes closed, but already he gyrated his hips softly, as if he were begging with them. Trent continued to torment his taut buds as he kissed his way up Shawn's throat until he reached the sweetness of his lips. Moaning as Trent took his mouth, it was clear that Shawn was more than ready to breach him, Shawn's hard length bumping his sac as they sloshed in the Jacuzzi.

He reached for the lube and Shawn broke their kiss, grabbing his arm.

"Not yet. I'm tasting you, remember?"

Trent swallowed. He remembered. Somehow he'd thought they'd be in bed when it happened, not in his yard.

"Stand up and face away from me."

If any of my neighbors see us…

It was unusual for him to allow a man to guide the action in the bedroom, to let someone else take command of his body. But Shawn was too sexy, made everything so erotic. He couldn't say no.

Rising out of the water, he did as Shawn had instructed. He almost fell forward when Shawn grasped his cheeks forcefully, parting them. A groan escaped him when Shawn blew on his hole. He felt himself clench, his shaft swollen with his need, twitching with each hot breath on his pucker.

"Shawn, please…"

The hardened point of Shawn's tongue nudged his opening, probing, seeking entrance. He relaxed into the sensation and Shawn breached him.

"God. *Damn*. So good."

Over and over Shawn pushed in. If he hadn't held onto him so well, Trent was sure he would've fallen forward. He rutted into air as Shawn licked at his insides, keeping his rim stretched with his hot, wet tongue. Clenching his fists at his sides, he didn't dare touch his dick in any way. He'd shoot immediately.

Shawn pulled out, but kept one hand on his hip.

"Don't move. I wanna stretch you more."

Shawn let go and Trent heard some shuffling around, the water splashing. His backside was parted again and the cool liquid of the lube made him jump. He was grateful. He'd been too close. One of Shawn's fingers invaded his passage, sliding in to the first knuckle. Shawn twisted it around and the urge to touch himself was almost unbearable.

"More."

A moan was Shawn's only answer and it ramped up the heat of the moment to know Shawn was as turned on as he was. Shawn added another digit and in addition to the swirl, he scissored them. He used his other hand to steady Trent, holding onto his hip to keep him from pitching forward as his thrusts became more forceful.

His cock leaked—a tiny string of pre-cum trailing off the end of his tip. Shawn dug deeper, reaching his gland and stroking it gently, causing sparks of electricity to shoot up his spine and to the end of his dick. It was too much, yet not enough. Right as he thought Shawn had finished finger fucking him, he added a third one and twisted his hand as he thrust in and out.

"Now. Inside me now."

He turned in time to see Shawn scoot up onto the edge of the Jacuzzi where he'd obviously padded the surface with the soft towels. Shawn had removed the condom from the packet and it lay in the palm of his hand.

"Put it on me."

He sucked in a breath and plucked the rubber from where it lay in Shawn's hand. After rolling it on his lover, he leaned in for a kiss. He was hungry for him, for their connection. As soon as Shawn was covered, he positioned himself over him and allowed Shawn to guide his cock to his entrance. He sank down on Shawn's thick column of flesh, impaling himself to the hilt.

Remaining still, he gazed down at Shawn. There was a look of awe in his eyes.

"This good for you?"

Shawn nodded shakily, his lips parted.

"Been years. Really good. You too?"

"Yes." Trent gave him a peck on his nose. "Wonderful."

"Lower us into the water."

Trent smiled. "Could get messy."

"That okay?"

In answer, he grasped Shawn's ass cheeks and lifted him keeping them connected. Once he had Shawn settled on the tub's ledge, he placed one hand at the small of his back to keep him from being hurt as he rode him. He used the other to brace himself against the edge of the Jacuzzi. Slowly, he moved on and off Shawn's cock.

The water sloshed with each motion, gradually creating waves that poured over the side onto the patio. He didn't give a shit, he was in heaven. The angle he needed to peg himself was difficult to achieve, but if he leaned back slightly, Shawn's dick would glance over his gland. He clutched the edge and grasped Shawn's shoulder to keep his balance.

Their shared moans filled the air. As much as he wanted to be quiet since they were outside, he wasn't sure it would be possible. Not when Shawn felt so incredible filling him, joining with him. Shawn's fingers curled around his aching member, jacking it. Trent made more space by arching his back to peg himself even more.

"Shawn…"

Unable to continue, he released on a strangled cry, clamping down on Shawn's cock so hard, he almost expelled him from his body.

"Oh, *Jesus*."

Shawn let go on a long moan, pulsing inside him. It stimulated him more, forcing more cum out of him.

The heat of the water and their urgent coupling had him dizzy, breathless.

Shawn sighed. "Baby, hold me. I need you."

He opened his eyes and leaned forward, his heart clutching at the vulnerability in Shawn's expression. He wrapped his arms around him, pulling him close, kissing his head, the side of his face. Shawn nuzzled into his neck, his hot breath fanning his skin. He'd never had anyone call him baby before. He decided he liked it.

They stayed in one another's arms as long as they could. When Shawn finally slipped free of his body, he grabbed for the condom. Shawn got to it first and they both laughed.

"How's your knee?"

"Fine. My tailbone however…"

As soon as Shawn winced, Trent leaped off him, sending another large wave of water sloshing onto the patio.

"I didn't mean for you to—"

"I'm taking over. Grab my hand."

He easily yanked Shawn up with one arm then pulled him close again, cradling him, stroking his lower back.

"I'm sorry. You should've said something."

"Not a chance. I didn't want you to stop."

"Don't do that again."

"I can't fuck you again?"

Not a half hour before he would have likely said he didn't want to be fucked again, or at least only on rare occasions. But he no longer felt that way. Not with Shawn. He'd made it a nut busting rollercoaster ride.

"Fucking me is a definite yes. You being hurt while fucking me is a definite no."

"I told you, I'm—"

"Fine. I know. I just can't stomach you being hurt in any way."

Shawn stared at him, a look of contemplation on his face.

"You're very serious about that, aren't you?"

"I've told you that before."

"I know. It just really hit me somehow when you said it this time."

"Well, it's true. I really care about you."

Trent wasn't used to a lot of things that he'd been experiencing with Shawn. However, openly sharing his feelings—especially when things were still so new—had to top everything else. Shawn appeared completely at ease with his words.

"I'm glad to hear that, since I really care about you too."

They kept their eyes locked on one another, no more words needed. Somehow, he was able to let himself be vulnerable with Shawn. It was also new for him, but it was okay. He was finding out that there were plenty of things that were okay with Shawn in his life.

"I'm taking you inside now. I want you to rest."

Shawn's amused smirk didn't escape his notice. He was aware that Shawn thought he was bossy, but he'd also noticed that his lover seemed to enjoy it most of the time. As much as he liked taking care of him, he was certain Shawn craved being taken care of sometimes. Even if it was only in the bedroom, Trent believed it was a significant part of their dynamic together.

"Come lie with me."

He went to grasp Shawn's hand but he pulled it back. Right as Trent was about to say something, Shawn wrapped his arms around his neck.

"My knee is bothering me. I might need you to carry me."

Yes. He would carry Shawn anytime.

* * * *

He still had to make sure to keep his knee wrapped, but at least he was back on duty. Their weekend together had been incredible—sex, driving to the mountains, more sex, eating at a UFO-themed diner, sex, a movie night, sex and finally, sex. His balls had actually ached in protest by Monday morning.

It was another Tuesday night—a week since he'd made a fool of himself by crashing to the ground in front of everyone. It was a maneuver he hoped never to repeat again. Trent would be off his shift by noon the next day and they'd already made plans to grab a quick lunch together before Shawn had to report back to the station.

"How's that knee?"

He was brought back to the present by Vicki's question. It was the longest he'd been on it since it had been injured. He had to admit it was bothering him somewhat and he'd noticed he'd fallen into a limp over the past hour.

"It's fine."

"Uh-huh. Don't make it worse by pushing yourself too soon."

Shawn harrumphed. "As if you should talk."

"Do as I say, not as I do."

"Nice."

He halted in order to focus on some type of disturbance a couple of yards ahead. Something was clearly wrong. People were pointing, covering their mouths, some running away, yelling. He caught Vicki's eye and they ran toward the chaos.

They could smell it right away, even before they got closer. Thick clouds of smoke, blacker than the backdrop of the night, poured onto the Strip. It came from the construction site of a new casino in the process of being built. Several older businesses had been torn down to create space for the new contender on the Boulevard.

It wasn't nearly as grand as some of the other hotels, but it was at least twenty stories high. It was midway through its construction, so there were large sections that were still in the skeletal stage. An open area in front of it remained unpaved—no doubt it would eventually be filled with fountains and other statements of grandeur. The sign at the front of the property proclaimed it to be the new home of Dark Fantasy, a vampire horror-themed venue.

Both he and Vicki worked to keep the crowds back. Sirens screamed in the distance and Shawn was certain there'd be more than one company called to battle the blaze. Already large flames curled around the edges of the building as if trying to embrace it. An older woman grabbed his arm.

"There's a man in that trailer. He stays there overnight to keep watch. I sometimes bring him coffee."

Shawn trained his gaze where the woman pointed. He could vaguely see the outline of the rectangular structure she was referring to. It was much too close to the fire.

"Why do you think he's still in there?"

He couldn't imagine the guy not noticing such a thing happening right next to him.

She looked sheepish. "He takes sleeping pills. Otherwise he says the noise on the Strip keeps him awake."

Awesome security system.

He turned to Vicki, but she cut him off before he could speak.

"Go ahead. Darren and Parker just pulled up, they can help me with crowd control."

He nodded then took off at a fast clip, mindful of the uneven ground. He'd almost expected her to insist that she go in his place because of his knee, but they were alike in the sense that he never would have insinuated she couldn't handle herself in a situation. He knew she would never make that decision for him either.

The smoke was much thicker the closer he got. He pulled the neck of his undershirt up so that it covered his mouth and nose. Right as he reached the door of the watchman's trailer, several loud pops exploded above the roar of the now-raging fire. Glass shattered around him and he knew it was imperative that he be quick. The place was locked up tight. He didn't have time to fuck around, so he took out his baton and bashed the flimsy handle of the door.

After minimal effort, he broke his way in. Sure enough, the loud snores of the security guard could be heard over the conflagration right outside. The structure was small and awkward. He wormed his way in, anxious to get them both out of there. As soon as he'd opened the trailer to the outside elements, it had begun filling with smoke.

It proved fruitless to wake the seemingly unconscious man, so he had no choice but to drag him out. Fortunately, he was slightly built and not very big. Still, it was unwieldy extracting them both from the crowded space as he coughed and sputtered. As soon as he'd exited, he felt a strong hand on his shoulder.

He whipped around and saw that it was Lee. He was in full gear, mask in place, so he gestured for Shawn to go back to the street. Shawn nodded in understanding and Lee picked up the still sleeping watchman and tossed him over his shoulder. They made their way through the tangle of hoses and other firefighters working their way toward the burning hotel.

As they reached the edge of the property, he spotted Trent next to his captain. They appeared to be involved in a heated discussion. Trent had his mask and tank in his arms, but wasn't in the process of putting them on. He didn't want to interfere with Trent while he was on the job, so he searched through the crowds to locate Vicki. She wasn't immediately visible, so he reached for his radio to contact her. He coughed loudly, the smoke still getting to him a bit.

"What the fuck did you think you were doing?"

He jumped at the sound of Trent's loud voice. Trent was right in his face and looked infuriated. He grabbed Shawn by the arms and shook him.

"Are you trying to give me a heart attack?"

What had always been a sexy growl was instead filled with anger. It was nothing like the Trent he knew. He stood speechless, not sure what to do or say. His Captain clapped his hand on Trent's shoulder and he shook it off.

Oh shit.

Trent was in big trouble, he could see it on his boss's face. Shawn tried to diffuse things until they could have a rational conversation away from work.

"I'm okay. Everything's fine."

Trent let Shawn go, dropping his hands to his sides. His face was still twisted in rage, but there was also hurt there, as if he was a wounded animal.

"Everything's not fine. Not fine, don't you understand? I can't do this." He shook his head—wouldn't stop. "I won't do this, not again. I'm done."

"What? What are you talking about?"

It hit him right then what Trent was saying. He meant that *they* were done. Trent was actually breaking up with him in the middle of a crowd in front of their peers during a major fire. He couldn't believe it. Couldn't move. Couldn't respond. Trent wouldn't even meet his eyes.

While all that had gone on between them, his Captain had stepped away. He reappeared with the Fire Marshal.

"Alan's giving you a ride back to the station, Trent. We'll discuss this further when I get back." He turned to Shawn. "Thank you for your quick action, but we've got everything under control now."

The Captain was politely dismissing him. As much as he had his own anger inside over what Trent had just done, he wanted to reach out to him, talk with him. He knew whatever was going on was related to his fears about what had happened with Paul, but he couldn't reconcile how extreme he'd reacted. For him to endanger his position at work, something else had to be going on.

A lump formed in his throat at the thought that Trent might actually mean what he'd said about them being done, but he told himself it couldn't be. They'd been so happy, growing so close. There had been discussions about Trent's need to protect him, his fears, but that had all seemed to have been worked out. He spotted Vicki.

He was aware that the confrontation between him, Trent and the Captain hadn't gone unnoticed. Those emergency workers still gathered around pretended not to see him, but he was mindful of them glancing his way. Maintaining his composure as best as he could, he walked toward his partner. Her expression almost did him in. She had compassion etched on her face. It made him think that what Trent had said must be true. That he really was done.

The last thing he was about to do was fall apart in public, so he cast his gaze to the ground. He couldn't risk losing control. She reached him but thankfully didn't mention anything about Trent.

"Just got a call about some working girls who were trespassing at The Venetian. They're still lingering around the front. Management wants us to talk to them."

Shawn nodded, looking down the expanse of the Las Vegas Strip. His new city, new beat. It was filled with wild, crazy and happy people most of the time. Opulence and splendor surrounded him. But there was an undercurrent of decay that the casual observer or temporary guest didn't notice. The sadness of people who lost themselves to a gambling addiction—alcoholism, drug overdoses. People selling their bodies to survive or to try to cash in on big money. Lovers torn apart by a bullet. A man unable to let go and find happiness again.

Perhaps Vegas was no different than Los Angeles. It was merely dressed up prettier.

Chapter Eight

He hadn't slept even one minute. Wasn't sure when he ever would again. Fire and Rescue had returned from the hotel incident and had informed him that the Captain was still wrapping things up. It was difficult to decide who he was more anxious about facing—his boss or his best friend. They were both going to tear into him.

At least Lee can't take my job away.

But it wasn't his job that ate away at him. It was his words, his behavior toward Shawn that gripped his insides and wouldn't let go. For almost an hour after he'd been deposited back at the station by the marshal, he'd been in the same state as he'd been at the fire. Overcome with anger at Shawn for putting himself in harm's way once again. It had been combined with the terror he'd experienced when he'd spotted Shawn running toward the flames without any protection.

The engine had barely slowed when he'd jumped down, ready to tear after his lover. Lee had been the first to try to stop him, but the Captain had stepped in.

He'd needed Lee to do what Trent wasn't doing—his job. By the time Shawn had returned from saving the security guard, Trent and the Captain had been arguing.

'You're here to do a specific task, one that doesn't involve you rescuing your lover who has his own responsibilities to the Force. I'm not putting up with this anymore. We're going to have a serious discussion about your future with the department when all this is over.'

Then he'd unleashed all of his frustration on Shawn. Pushed him away. Told him in so many words that they were finished. He could feel the emotion welling up inside him at the thought of losing Shawn in a different way than what drove his fears. It wasn't fair to keep pulling the shit on him that he did. He deserved more than that. Shawn was a hard-working police officer with a promising career ahead of him. He didn't need a boyfriend with emotional baggage continuously humiliating him, treating him as though he were incapable.

He winced at the truth of his own thoughts. Would he want someone inferring that *he* couldn't do his job, that *he* was incompetent? That was what he'd been doing to Shawn and his lover had put up with him anyway. He cared about Shawn a lot like he'd told him. It was obvious to Trent that he had some serious issues to work out before he could really be with anyone. Until then, it was best for all involved if he stayed alone.

The rumble of the garage door downstairs heralded the return of the engine. He collected his mug that had held old coffee in it to take to the sink. All he'd done since returning from the scene was sit in the kitchen, drinking the vile brew, mulling things over. The TV had provided an occasional mild distraction, but his thoughts had drifted to moments with Shawn—ones he might not ever experience again.

Footsteps sounded on the stairs and he knew he had hell to pay. It was after four o'clock in the morning, so he wasn't sure what to expect. Lee, Jamal and Ed poured in, Captain Sawyer on their heels. Everyone filed past him, none meeting his eyes—not even Lee. The Captain stopped when he got to him. He reeked of smoke, his eyes red rimmed. It was clear the man was exhausted.

"Go to bed, Marshall. I'm not doing this now. Be in my office at ten in the morning, got it?"

"Yes, sir."

He rinsed out his cup and put it in the dish drainer. Glancing toward the sleeping area, he contemplated trying to get some rest. The thought of going in the room he typically shared with Lee and Jamal left him queasy. He turned and considered the couch. At least in there he could let the bad television lull him into numbness.

The couch it was.

* * * *

Multiple texts and voicemails had gone unanswered in the week since Trent had exploded at him in front of everyone. Shawn had wavered back and forth between anger and misery. The emotion that currently took precedence over the other two was sadness. He'd assumed that after Trent had calmed down, they'd have a chance to talk. That didn't appear to be the case.

He'd found out through Vicki that Trent was on 'vacation'. She'd confided in him that the talk she'd heard centered on it being a forced vacation. It explained why Shawn hadn't run into him at all during the week, despite Station 32 being called out to a number of incidents where he'd been present. Despite some of the anger he still held inside about what Trent had done, he also had some twinges of guilt. Although he knew he wasn't responsible for Trent getting in trouble, the fact that he'd been the inadvertent cause of it made him feel bad.

He'd decided to take a few days off to get his head back on straight. There hadn't been an opportunity to do so any sooner. But the new recruits needed some on-the-job training and Vicki had volunteered to partner up. That had allowed him to request a couple of vacation days. So far, his plan to pull himself together hadn't been very successful. All it had done was give him the chance to contemplate why the deterioration of such a new relationship had hit him so hard.

I'm falling in love with the fucker.

Their last weekend together had definitely been lust-driven, but there had also been a lot more to it than sex. There was an ease and comfort he'd never experienced with anyone before Trent. A natural, unforced compatibility. A mind-blowing connection. That triggered the anger in him again. Was Trent that stupid that he would toss all that away over the risks Shawn took because of his job?

It wasn't that he was unmindful of the agony Trent had gone through because of Paul's murder in the line of duty. But Trent had acknowledged that he'd been overreacting and had assured him he'd work on it.

His cell went off and he picked it up, wondering if he was being called in after all. He'd let the department know he wasn't leaving town, that he was only going on a 'staycation'. Checking the caller ID, he almost dropped the phone. It was Trent. His hands shook and he waited so long to answer it, the phone went to voicemail. He stared at it. Contemplating. Questioning.

His first instinct had been to call him right back, not even listen to the message. He'd stopped himself though after thinking about it. It would be such a girl move, one he'd never had the urge to do before.

The gym. Head to the gym. Shake it off.

After throwing some workout clothes in his bag, he blasted out of there, anxious to let go of the compulsion to chase after Trent. The hour and a half he worked himself into a lather did take the edge off. If nothing else, it knocked the wind out of him enough that he wasn't as desperate to talk to Trent. Sort of.

He reflexively checked his cell. No new calls. There was a message that he knew was from Trent. He frowned at his evil phone. It stared back at him, mocking.

Perfect. I'm losing my mind.

Gathering his things, he thought he would see if Vicki might want to meet up for lunch or coffee. He needed to speak his thoughts out loud and she'd be the perfect sounding board for that. There was a lot to be said for blunt.

He waited until he got to his Rav4 so he could keep the conversation private. Even though he knew it was her day off, he had no idea whether she had any plans or not. He turned on the AC while he sat in the SUV so he wouldn't fry while he called. She picked up right away.

"Feeling social?"

"In a manner of speaking. You had lunch yet?"

"No." She sighed. "I can see where this is going. You buying?"

He snorted. "Sure. Can I use you as my fake therapist?"

"Why not. As much as I was really looking forward to doing the laundry, I suppose it could wait. Ernie's Taqueria?"

"I'm not that far. I'll head over now. Whenever you can get there is fine."

"Order me an iced tea."

"Yes, ma'am."

"Asshole."

They hung up and he headed to the downtown area. It was more old school and the casinos much smaller—but just as colorful. He'd been there less than fifteen minutes when Vicki arrived. They went through the motions of ordering some food and making small talk while they ate. She'd finished her taquitos and leaned back in her chair, nibbling on some of the chips from the basket between them. He'd spent the majority of the time poking and prodding his soft fish tacos. They were his favorite, but his stomach hadn't stopped turning all week.

"Out with it."

"Sorry."

"Fuck that. What's the Trent update?"

He sighed before he could stop himself. He glanced up in time to see her narrow her eyes at him.

"There's not much to tell. I've sent several texts and left a couple messages since last week and he didn't respond. Until today."

"And?"

"I let it go to voicemail."

"And?"

"Jesus. I don't know, I didn't listen to it."

"This is the most boring update I've ever heard. Washing my *chones* would've been more interesting."

"Please. No underwear stories."

"Why am I here, Shawn? It's obvious you wanna talk about something. And you look pathetic. Just sayin'."

He frowned at her, but knew she was right all the same.

"I want him so bad, miss him. I don't want things to end. He never gave us a real chance."

"And I'm sure he realizes that."

"But what if he called to tell me to leave him alone? That we were really over and to quit bugging him?"

"You are such a girl."

He cringed. "Yeah. I'd been thinking that too."

"Then get over yourself and listen to the voicemail."

"But what if—?"

"Pigs fly? Could happen. In the meantime, deal with this. It's not going to go away. If he's too stubborn or messed up to see love right in front of him, then he's not worth your effort."

He almost gasped. "Love? I never said—"

"Oh shut up. Check your voicemail."

Staring down at his mangled lunch, he knew she was right about everything. He met her eyes. Now that he had the chance to talk things out with her, he was anxious to get home to listen to the voicemail. He wanted to be alone in case it said something he didn't want to hear.

"So get outta here."

Giving her a grateful look, he rose from his chair.

"Thanks Vicki. I really appreciate it."

"Hey, anytime you wanna buy me lunch is fine. Next time try not to do it when you're so mopey though."

He chuckled. "It's a deal."

* * * *

The drive back from the taqueria was tension packed. He was anxious to hear what Trent had to say and terrified all at once. Meeting with Vicki had been the right call, though. As he pulled onto his street, he could swear that Trent's red truck was parked in front of his building.

I'm really reaching now.

He almost slammed on the brakes when he spotted Trent in the vehicle. He had his head bowed, after which he glanced up, facing forward. It was obvious he hadn't noticed Shawn. His brake lights went on, indicating he was about to pull away. Without thinking, Shawn honked his horn.

Trent's head whipped around and they locked eyes for a brief moment. Shawn held up a finger as he drove slowly past, hoping Trent understood that he wanted him to wait—that he would wait. He was in forward motion, deciding he would save the musings over whether he was acting too eager for later.

By the time he'd parked in the underground garage and made his way to the front, Trent was leaning against the wall right outside the security doors. Instantly, his heart seemed to jump into his throat, and his breathing sped up. He wanted to shake his hands out, deplete some of his nervous energy, but Trent was already looking his way.

As he opened the door for Trent, he had to avert his gaze. Where he'd desired to be open and vulnerable to him before, it felt too dangerous under the current circumstances. He dared to lift his head and catch his eyes long enough to not come across as if he were a beaten dog.

"Do you wanna come in?"

"I'd like that very much."

He swallowed, still unsure, but hopeful. Without answering, he turned then made his way to his apartment. His fucking hands wouldn't stop trembling as he unlocked his apartment door and he inwardly cursed himself for being so foolish. So susceptible to the man standing right behind him.

After tossing his keys on the small kitchen counter, he gestured for Trent to sit. He rubbed his hands through his hair before turning around. He *hated* uncomfortable confrontations with people who mattered to him. There hadn't been many instances—or people—where he'd had to deal with it, but the one he was about to face with Trent was the absolute worst. No one had ever mattered so much.

Trent sat on a cushioned chair next to the sofa, perched on the edge with his hands clasped in front of him. He was clearly ill at ease.

"Did you get my voicemail?"

"No."

Even though Shawn wished for a positive outcome, he wouldn't make it easy for him. Shawn wasn't the one who had the issues.

"I understand." Trent's gaze flitted around the room, he seemed at a loss.

"Why are you here?"

Nodding, Trent finally lifted his eyes to Shawn's. He forced himself not to back away from Trent's silently pleading look.

"I'm sorry."

Shawn was about to speak when a surge of emotions crashed through him. He took a few deep breaths, his control slipping away. He couldn't hold back.

"*Sorry*? You're kidding, right?"

Shawn turned away, grabbing the counter to keep himself from slamming his fist on it. As much as he hoped they could work it out, *longed* for it, a simple sorry wasn't going to cut it. He'd heard Trent's apologies before and a new one wasn't about to impress him. They'd obviously not been enough to keep Trent from falling apart at the first sign of trouble.

"I know, Shawn. I know. Would you let me explain why I believe it's different this time? If you think I'm full of shit, then I'll leave. I won't bother you anymore."

Shawn pressed his lips together, his anger still swirling around in his gut. After all the agony he'd been through for the past week, he should at least give Trent a chance. Give them both a chance.

He lowered his arms to his side then dragged himself to the couch. He dropped down, not sure what Trent could possibly say to make him believe things could change. During the entire week he'd tried to reach Trent to talk things out, he'd never stopped to consider that there might not be a way for Trent to handle being in a relationship with him, that he might've been right to break it off.

He'd purposely sat at the other end of the sofa, safely out of range from Trent's touch. If he touched him, there was a good chance he'd give in to anything Trent proposed.

"Fine. Convince me."

"I'm seeing someone."

Shawn almost choked then sputtered out a disgusted laugh. "You're insane. How's going out with someone else going to inspire me to forgive you? Is that the only reason you came over here today…"

"Shawn…"

"To prove to me that you're a changed man, hoping I'll forgive you so that you can clear your conscience and move on..."

"*Shawn...*"

"With your new lover?"

"A therapist. I'm seeing a *therapist*."

He shook his head in confusion. "You're dating a therapist?"

Trent dropped his head in one hand, rubbing his forehead. At last he rose from the chair and moved toward Shawn as if he were about to hug him. Shawn angled back and held his hands up in front of him. Trent sat down on the end of the couch, appearing contrite.

"She thinks I have PTSD. Captain Taylor gave me an ultimatum. He strongly suggested I take my vacation time and get some professional help or he was going to bring me up before the board to review my actions at the hotel fire."

Shawn arched his eyebrows in surprise. It wasn't at all what he'd expected from the man of few words he'd been falling for. There was no doubt it had to have been a difficult thing for him to do. Although, he supposed the threat of losing his livelihood had been a major motivator.

"Um. Good. I think that's a good thing. However, I don't see why you needed to come over here and tell me. Don't get me wrong, I wish you all the best. I hope this gets you the help you need. But I was already too emotionally invested into us as a couple, and I can't be there for you as just a friend. I'm sorry."

"I don't want just a friend."

Shawn let his head fall back on the cushion. He couldn't help but wonder if the therapist had been stuck doing all the talking. Finally, he angled his body to face Trent. He needed him to get to the point.

"Can you practice your newfound desire to speak about your deepest feelings on me? I don't understand what you're really trying to say to me and after all the suffering I've been through this past week, I'm not in the mood to guess."

Trent furrowed his brow, pressing his lips together. The man seemed to be struggling.

"I'm trying to say that I'm getting help in the hopes that I can build a life with you, so that I can be everything you need from a man. I care about my job, but I'd already thought about moving away from Vegas if you weren't going to be in my life any longer. I wouldn't be able to handle being here, seeing you on calls, aching for you."

Holy crap.

"I…uh…" Yeah. He couldn't believe what he was hearing. "Really?"

He couldn't mask his disbelief. Not that he didn't doubt what Trent was saying. The one thing he'd always had complete confidence in was that Trent was an honest man. It was simply that it hadn't been anywhere near to what he'd thought he was going to say.

"Really. Please Shawn, I've never begged before. But I'm begging you now. Give me another chance. If you want, I'll agree to counseling together, whatever it takes to make you comfortable with giving us another try."

It was easy for him to respond. "Okay. But I have one condition."

"Whatever you want."

"You might want to hear my condition first."

"I don't give a fuck what it is. Anything you want."

"Wow. All right then, no sex. No being alone at either of our places until we meet with your therapist a few times. Then we'll see."

Trent nodded, swallowing a couple of times before he answered. "Agreed."

That had gone over better than he'd anticipated. They sat in silence, not yet fully comfortable with one another.

"Are you working tomorrow?"

Shawn inhaled deeply, hoping that whatever it was Trent had in mind he would want to agree to it.

"No, I took some vacation days."

Trent had a pained look on his face. "I see. In that case, I have an appointment with Dr Silver. Would you like to join me?"

The man didn't waste any time. "Sure. What time?"

"Two o'clock. If you're okay with it, I can either pick you up, or we could meet at the diner for some lunch ahead of time." He paused. "Or we can just meet at her office."

Shawn considered the options. "I think for this time I'd rather have my own vehicle. But I'll meet you at the diner."

The tension visibly drained from Trent's face. "Thank you." He ran his hand through his hair. "Can I hold you before I go?"

Shawn bit his bottom lip. God, how he wanted Trent to hold him. But he couldn't allow Trent anywhere near him while they were alone. He didn't trust himself in the slightest.

"I'll walk you out. When we get to your truck…then, yes. I'd like that."

They were silent as they made their way to Trent's vehicle, Trent holding the front security door open for him. Shawn nodded to him in acknowledgment, his nerves rising, threatening to overtake him. Once they reached his truck, he turned to face Trent.

The pained expression had returned and Shawn longed to comfort him. But it was smart to take things slow.

"I really am sorry, Shawn."

Shawn nodded again and Trent gathered him in a hug. They held on to each other tight, no words, no caresses. He breathed in Trent's masculine aroma, melted into the warm strength that was his lover.

My lover.

And so much more.

Chapter Nine

Trent had shown up at the diner early to gather his thoughts and hopefully calm himself before Shawn arrived. He'd been a wound up ball of nerves all night and it had not only carried through into the next day, but had amped up on his drive to the restaurant. He and Dr Silver had already discussed whether he had transferred his feelings for Paul onto Shawn, creating a bond that wasn't actually there.

After a couple of sessions with her he'd been able to work out that his fears had nothing to do with that. Shawn was actually quite different from Paul in looks, temperament and he had to admit, sexual drive. He loved Shawn exactly the way he was and had no desire to change, or mold him into a replica of Paul or their lost relationship. She'd also suggested that he keep any declarations of love to himself for the time being. It would place too much pressure on Shawn, and she also felt Trent should take some more time to sit with those feelings before saying them out loud.

The idea that he would get any benefit out of going to a therapist had been the biggest surprise to him, amongst everything else. When Lee had gently suggested he seek help after Paul's death, he'd scoffed at the whole idea. He hadn't believed in airing his innermost feelings to some stranger. He was barely capable of it with people he knew very well, and even then, in a very limited basis. But with the threat of losing everything he cared about looming over him, he'd finally given in.

When the front bell jangled on the door to the restaurant, he glanced up. His heart fluttered at the sight of Shawn walking toward him. It would take all his willpower not to reach for him. As he approached, he noted the slight discomfort evident in Shawn's body language.

"Hey," he said, as he slid into the booth across from Trent.

"Hi Shawn. Thank you for meeting me for lunch."

Shawn cleared his throat in what seemed to be his own nervousness. They'd never been so uncomfortable with one another, even in the beginning.

"I'm glad we could get together before…um, the appointment."

Lora strolled over to the table, the book of paper order tickets in her hand, her pencil poised.

"Are you guys ready, or do you need a minute?"

Trent looked at Shawn, deferring to him.

Shawn turned to her.

"We'll have the usual."

The couple of times they'd eaten there, the turkey and avocado sandwich had been their mutual choice. But Trent was the one that usually ordered for them. Once she'd written their choices down, she walked away. They were left to their own devices. As Trent ran through possible non-conflict inducing topics of conversation in his mind, Shawn spoke up.

"I don't suppose you've heard any news regarding the cause of the hotel fire?"

That had been the one subject he'd planned on studiously avoiding sans therapist, but as long as Shawn was willing to talk about it, he would gladly go along.

"I spoke with Lee on the phone briefly." He paused, realizing that he was self-editing everything in his head, not allowing himself to converse naturally. Even if he wasn't verbose, he never overthought his words. "He was checking on me. Uh, he mentioned that the same group who'd claimed responsibility for the other incidents was claiming it again."

"Yeah, I'd thought that would be the case. I haven't asked Vicki about it, but I'm betting the department is under a lot of pressure to solve this thing fast. The last thing Vegas wants is for tourists to be scared off. What about that briefing? Any news on that?"

Trent shifted in his seat. "I'm not…I haven't been included in anything regarding what's going on there."

"Oh. I see."

Lora arrived with their teas and they sipped them in silence, Trent was unable to stop himself from fiddling with his spoon like he always did. He focused on pushing his frightened emotions aside and bringing his mind back around to the man seated before him—the reason he was going through so much effort to straighten himself out.

"Did you ever upload the pictures from Spring Mountain?"

Shawn's eyes seemed to light up. "Actually, yeah. There are a few shots that came out amazing, I'm thinking of getting them printed, maybe framed. I don't know, but I can't wait for you to see them, tell me what you think." The words had tumbled out of Shawn almost breathlessly, but he appeared to catch himself. "I mean, you know…at some point."

Trent nodded with a tight smile. It would take some time.

"I'd like that. I'd like it a lot."

He took another drink of tea then set the glass, covered in condensation, down. Playing a finger through the moisture, he tried not to fall back into fear. He raised his eyes and Shawn's gaze was there to meet them, no hesitation.

"Were they the ones you took of those Yellow Orioles?"

"Some of them. But there was also a nice one I caught of you by the ranch house."

A smile spread across Shawn's face, and Trent relaxed in the booth, exhaling as he did.

He could feel it. They were going to be okay.

* * * *

So far, he'd gone to two sessions with Trent. After the lunch at the diner, they'd also had dinner one night and gone to a movie on another. There was no doubt Trent had experienced a change within himself and Shawn had been worried at first—worried that it might mean that Trent would decide to move on without him or that they wouldn't fit together in the same way they had before. It was selfish, but he'd come to the conclusion that he really *did* want to be a part of Trent's life. His feelings had only intensified.

Relating to one another without the sex had also been disconcerting, but he was gladder than ever he'd made that a provision. They had no choice but to communicate with one another on a basic level—there wasn't the anticipation of what they'd do together later driving their interaction. It was only about them enjoying each other's company.

Who knew?

He'd even decided that he really liked Dr Silver. He wanted to give her a million dollars for helping Trent so much in such a short time. Because truthfully, the changes in Trent were very positive and he'd reached the conclusion that they most definitely were a good thing. She'd reminded them both that it would still take time and not to expect miracles. But she'd also given them an outlet if things became too much. Trent knew he had someone to vent to if he got out of control and Shawn knew he could set boundaries with Trent without the fear of losing him.

Now, about that sex thing…

They had another appointment in the morning. They'd have to squeeze it in before Shawn went back to work. The following day, Trent would be returning to the fire station for the first time since his mandated vacation, so there wouldn't be any nooky coming their way soon.

He reclined on his sofa, catching up on the news, eating an apple. A breaking news story popped in and he straightened up. The announcer stated that a prostitute had been murdered. That part was unfortunately all too common and rarely hit the airwaves. The other aspect of the story was what had chilled his blood. The same Citizens Against Immorality had claimed responsibility.

His phone went off and he grabbed it, answering even as he brought it to his ear. He heard Trent's voice.

"Turn on the local news."

"It's on."

Trent stopped talking, no doubt listening to the rest of the report right along with Shawn. As soon as it finished, Shawn pointed the remote at the TV and shut it off.

"Holy shit."

Trent grunted. "That's an understatement."

"God, what's happening to this town?"

"What's happening everywhere? People filled with hate, intent on forcing everyone else to follow their agenda, no matter the cost."

"Obviously they missed the part where hatred, and…uh, murder, is also immoral."

"Lee told me there haven't been any fires on the Strip or other attempts since the big hotel one. It looks like they've moved on to other more insidious activities."

"Or they were trying to dodge the extra attention paid to security that their repeated arson attempts had generated. With all agencies remaining hyper-alert to suspicious behavior related to fire prevention, maybe they went another route. I think it stands to reason that if they were willing to set fire to occupied buildings, they're not squeamish about taking lives."

"That seems to be a logical conclusion," Trent agreed. "Perhaps they'd hoped for deaths before this but when it didn't pan out, they went for a more direct route. It's chilling."

"I'm thinking I'll hear more when I go in tomorrow."

Trent was silent.

"You still there?"

"Yeah. I'm here…"

He paused and Shawn knew something was bothering him.

"Out with it."

"We're still on for tomorrow with Dr Silver?"

"Of course. Why?"

"I…"

Shawn was still getting used to Trent's less assured manner.

"I'm not someone to be afraid of Trent."

"Yes you are."

"Huh?"

"I'm afraid of losing you."

He sighed. "Trent, that's not likely to happen, judging by how things are going. I don't want to lose you either."

"You seemed okay with the sessions, but I wasn't sure."

"You could've asked."

"Working on it."

"I know. It's made a big difference already and…"

Should he say the next part?

"The next time we have the same day off, I was thinking…"

God, now who's having a hard time communicating?

He took a deep breath. "Maybe I could come over. If you want."

"Shawn."

He'd said it barely above a whisper and Shawn had a moment of trepidation where he thought he'd be rejected.

"I want that more than anything, Shawn. As long as you're sure you're ready. We don't need to rush anything."

"I'm ready."

He was too excited and didn't want to ruin the moment by saying something goofy.

"So I'll see you tomorrow, and we can discuss schedules then. Sound good?"

"Sounds perfect. Thank you, Shawn."

"Thank me when we're alone. You can make everything up to me then."

There was a definite groan from Trent. "I will, more than make it up."

"I'll be looking forward to that."

He ended the call with a nice boner for his trouble. Since he wouldn't be seeing Trent right away, he decided to go ahead and take care of it. He woke up his laptop that was on the coffee table in front of him. He went to his pictures' folder and brought up the photo of Trent standing by the red ranch house at Spring Mountain. He was looking toward one of the gnarled trees, his body angled in a way that his shorts hugged his glorious ass wonderfully. Trent's muscular thighs and calves were showcased below the hiking shorts and he had one hand on his hip that accentuated his biceps. His profile was beautiful and Shawn's cock was hot and swollen, he balls heavy in his sac. He began to stroke himself slowly, staring at Trent's picture.

He wouldn't last long.

* * * *

Stirring his coffee in the break room, Shawn mulled over the session he and Trent had had with Dr Silver earlier. Trent had blurted out that he'd asked to come over and Shawn had been pissed at him. Even though they'd shared the no sex rule at the initial meeting with the therapist, Shawn hadn't thought it necessary to ask her permission. Trent hadn't worded it that way, but it was how it'd felt.

Once they'd begun talking about it, Shawn had been glad that Trent had brought it up after all. By bringing their emotions out in the open, it had cleared the way even more for them. Shawn had left the session more convinced than ever that they were ready to be intimate again.

Vicki strolled into the room. "There you are. How're the meetings going with that person you were telling me about?"

After their lunch meeting that day and Trent's unexpected visit, he'd called and let her know what was going on. She'd been very encouraging.

"Really well. I think the problem's been handled and we're ready to move ahead."

She raised her eyebrows, sticking her out her bottom lip and nodding. "That so? Glad to hear it."

Darren stuck his head in the door. "Hey, the Lieutenant has called a meeting in the briefing room before we all head out tonight."

He and Vicki exchanged glances. There was little doubt that it pertained to the Citizens Against Immorality group. They grabbed their coffees then hurried down the hall to the conference area. When they arrived, the room was full, so they stood at the back, the buzz of voices a bit more excited than normal.

Lieutenant Campos stepped in and walked to the front of the room. He gestured for quiet and finally had everyone's attention.

"Okay, people, we all know that there's a group of unknowns in our city that's been setting fires and has now claimed to be behind last night's call girl murder. I won't go into all the details again. I think we're all aware of the basics. However, we're going to have to be even more vigilant when it comes to safety on the Boulevard.

"As with the other crimes, the murder came with a warning that more citizens would pay if the city wasn't cleansed of its evil. So we need you to take note of the people around you. Be aware of more than the ones causing trouble. Look for individuals that seem to always be around that feel out of place. The calls you're going to, do they seem legit, or are they distractions to keep our attention fixed elsewhere? Are the same people always on our radar? Anything that you can think of would be appreciated no matter how small, how insignificant it might seem. Gut feelings won't be discounted at this point."

He exhaled, weariness evident in the sound. "Good luck out there tonight. Carry on."

He and Vicki ran into Darren on the way to the garage.

"What do you guys think? I was almost wondering if it might not be a copycat."

Shawn considered Darren's theory. "Possibly. But if the lieutenant is taking gut instincts into consideration, I think it's all the same group. They've had a consistent pattern of targeting places—and a person—that specifically have a more obviously lurid theme. Burlesque, vampires, a known prostitute."

Darren nodded. "I can see that. Although, the entire town is referred to as Sin City. They've got a big job ahead of them if they want to stamp out everything they consider immoral."

Vicki made a very unladylike grunting noise. "No kidding."

Darren reached his cruiser, his partner Parker already waiting. They said their good-byes and he and Vicki went to their police-issued vehicle.

"Think there'll be a buttload of tourists filling the sidewalks tonight like usual?"

Vicki unlocked the car, frowning at him as she did. "You were thinking that one dead hooker would clear the streets?" She snorted. "Hardly. These people are here to party. They don't want any unpleasantness to intrude on their fun."

Shawn opened his door then got in. He had a sick feeling in his stomach. "Unpleasantness. I guess it's no different here than anywhere else."

Prostitutes were disposable victims. Society rarely worked too hard trying to discover who their killers were. Once in a while if it became known that a serial killer was on the loose, then a task force might be created. In which case, if the Citizens Against Immorality didn't feel they were getting enough attention or creating the proper fear in people, would they go after someone more likely to garner sympathy?

* * * *

It was almost strange to be back at the station. Other than Lee, he hadn't spoken to anyone else since he'd left. He dropped off his bag at his usual bunk assignment, then went down the hall to check in with Captain Taylor as he'd requested. He knocked softly on the slightly ajar door.

"Come in."

The Captain glanced up from his laptop screen and regarded him with an indifferent gaze. Now he knew how others felt when they'd accused him of having a stone face.

"Have a seat, Trent."

He swallowed hard, almost as if he were back in elementary school after getting caught writing on the walls. Once he'd lowered himself into the chair, he remained perched on the edge of it. The Captain arched one eyebrow.

"Relax. I'm not going to yell at you. Yet."

Trent nodded. "I appreciate that."

The Captain eased back in his chair and clasped his hands in front of him. "I gather from our conversation a few days ago that you feel you're ready to come back and be an effective member of the team?"

"Yes, sir. Like I said, the counseling sessions have been going very well and things with Shawn and I are working out in a way where I don't see it being an issue out in the field."

"And he's in agreement with what we discussed?"

"Yes, sir. He's agreed that we won't interact if we're both called out to the same incident."

"Good."

The Captain continued to stare at him as if he were contemplating whether or not to say anything else.

"Before you go, I want to add one more thing."

"Sir?"

"You're a good man, Trent—a good firefighter. You've built a solid career for yourself in Clark County and we're proud to have you on our team. It was a horrible thing that happened to Paul. I'm glad you're finally moving on with your life and you've found someone to care about. Don't fuck it up."

Trent gave Captain Taylor a tight smile. "Thank you, sir. I won't."

"Good. Making any dinner tonight? I don't think I can handle another vat of spaghetti from your buddy Lee out there."

"Pick up any chicken or veggies?"

"Both. There's also some rice, salad fixings and stuff to make turkey burgers."

"Sounds like we're set for the next couple days."

"Thank Christ. I don't know who's happier to have you back—me or my stomach."

This time, Trent couldn't stop himself from giving the Captain a genuine grin. "I'll work on keeping you both happy."

"Glad to hear it." He looked back down at his computer screen. "Well, get to work then."

Trent rose from the chair then headed straight for the kitchen. He spotted Lee digging around in the cupboards.

"What're you looking for?"

Still intent on his search, he answered Trent without turning toward him. "It's the weirdest thing. I could've sworn I had at least four or five jars of spaghetti sauce in here, but they're all missing."

Trent felt bubbles of laughter trying to force their way to the surface. He hadn't experienced such a lighthearted feeling for a while.

"Huh. Imagine that."

Lee straightened and whipped around to face him. He narrowed his eyes in suspicion.

"What do you know about my spaghetti sauce?"

"Me? I just got here."

"Mmmm. Something funny's going on here."

"Got paranoid since I've been gone?"

"I'm not paranoid, I'm just…inquisitive."

Trent grunted. "As long as you're sauce-less, why don't you get out of the way so I can rustle us all up something to eat?"

Lee pressed his lips together. "You know something. It was Jamal, right?"

Trent shook his head the way he always did. Some things hadn't changed. Lee must have thought he was reacting to his question.

"Okay, it was Ed then. Ben?"

"It was me."

They both turned to see Captain Taylor standing at the edge of the kitchen, his arms crossed in front of him.

"And for the record, I never want to see those jars of red shit in here ever again."

Lee scowled at him. "Hey, I didn't see anyone else volunteering to help in here."

The squabbling continued and Trent chuckled to himself. He was glad to be back. Really glad.

* * * *

So far, the evening patrol had been remarkable in its calm. The crowds were slightly less boisterous, somewhat less full. To an outsider, it would've appeared overflowing, packed. To someone who saw the same stretch of sidewalk every night, there was a marked difference.

"I never thought I'd say such a thing out here, but I'm actually bored."

"Yuppers. Me too."

Vicki ambled along, one hand resting on her duty belt, the other swinging lightly at her side. Regardless of the apparent calm, he knew they would both remain aware of their surroundings, never letting their guard down for a moment. As patrol partners, they were an excellent fit. They had an almost uncanny ability to vibe off one another. He could tell when she was out of sorts or distracted and she seemed to be able to do the same thing with him.

They passed by a street performer who was posed like a statue, completely still, his eyes closed. His entire face and body was covered in what looked like golden paint that sparkled. Even his clothing was the same color, reinforcing the impression that he was an actual statue. Tourists would walk by, uncertain, staring at him. Every once in a while, he would make a sudden move and change positions, eliciting yelps and shrieks of surprise. An upturned matching golden top hat was positioned on the ground next to him, ready to collect tips.

As they strolled by, Shawn happened to see the same woman who'd alerted him to the sleeping man in the trailer standing amongst the semicircle of observers.

"The one who would bring him coffee." He'd muttered it under his breath.

"Huh?" Vicki looked up and followed his gaze. "Oh, hey. That's the woman that was being attacked the night you fell."

He froze. "Oh, shit."

Not pausing to give Vicki an explanation, he elbowed his way through the crowd. He attempted to keep an eye on her, but she was short and by the time he reached the spot where she'd been standing not seconds before, she was gone. He turned to the couple next to him.

"Did you see where the woman went who was just here? Do you know her?"

They were practically hypnotized by the street performer, so barely reacted to him.

"What?" The man answered.

"The woman standing here just now. Do you know where she went?"

"What woman?"

Shawn frowned. "Never mind. Thanks."

The onlooker immediately went back to watching the statue man. Right then, Vicki caught up to him. He grabbed her arm.

"Call Darren and Parker, tell them to get right over here."

She didn't question—he knew she trusted him. As soon as she'd done what he requested, he stepped back from the group of people, staying in the shadows with his back to the casino behind them, observing.

"Fill me in."

"That woman you said was the one being attacked when I fell?"

"Yeah."

"She's the same one who came up to me the night of the hotel fire. The one who told me about the guy in the trailer."

"Damn. What're your thoughts?"

It had all caught him by surprise. He went over the various pieces in his mind, trying to put them together so they made sense.

Everyone is focused on the performer. They're not looking anywhere else. Even the people standing right next to that woman hadn't been aware she was there.

"Did anything else happen the night I fell? Any fires, anything that might have to do with the Citizen's group?"

"Uh, yeah actually. It wasn't too far from the motel, not long after you were hurt. It was at one of the big hotels. No real damage though."

"What if what happened was a distraction that was meant to keep emergency responders busy elsewhere?"

"But that was a genuine incident. A woman was being attacked and the other guy was caught."

"Didn't you say something about her getting a ride with someone rather than being transported?"

She furrowed her brow. "That sounds familiar."

Off to the left, he spotted Darren and Parker's cruiser drive into the half-moon driveway of the casino. They parked it to the side then got out, picking up a jog as they headed toward them.

"What's going on?" Darren cast his gaze around the area in what appeared to be an effort to remain on guard. "Vicki didn't give details."

He went through a brief explanation of what he'd told Vicki. They agreed to take the cruiser and see if they couldn't locate the woman that Shawn had described. After the two officers left, he and Vicki continued their patrol, hyper-aware of their surroundings and also on the lookout for the woman.

A piercing scream sounded behind them. It seemed to come from an area at the farthest end of the casino where they'd stood watching the street performer. They followed the desperate cry of the continuing scream down a walkway that led to a service entrance. Their senses were assailed by a combination of smoke and a sickeningly sweet smell. A young woman in a black minidress and heels raced toward them, shrieking and crying. Vicki lunged forward to grab her before she fell.

While that went on, Shawn radioed dispatch to send a fire crew. The smoke seemed minimal and was wafting from behind a dumpster. The woman Vicki held onto babbled hysterically.

"Offered me money, said to come back here, he... Oh God, she was already on fire."

Her feet gave way and she collapsed, Vicki lowering her to the ground. Shawn's stomach roiled and he caught Vicki's somber gaze. He raced to the dumpster on the slim chance there was still hope. He barely registered Vicki shouting for him not to go.

As soon as he rounded the corner and looked behind the large metal garbage bin, it was clear hope was long gone. A smoking, blackened corpse, unrecognizable as a human being lay on the ground. He covered his nose with the back of his hand, turning quickly away. He fought to keep from heaving.

The shrill sound of emergency vehicles approached and he purposefully walked away from what he knew was a crime scene. It would be a job for the detectives and CSI—as it was he might've already compromised the area in his futile attempt to help. As he got closer to Vicki, she raised her head, a questioning look on her face. He'd taken his hand away from his mouth and gave her a grim shake of his head.

He noted Ben and Jamal trotting over to where the woman lay unconscious on the ground next to Vicki. It meant Station 32 was the first on the scene. If Trent was there, everyone would be keeping a close eye on them, particularly Trent's Captain. A thought struck him.

Darren and Parker were nearby, the call for help drawing them back to the scene to assist in keeping onlookers back and to secure the crime scene until detectives arrived. He sidled over to where Darren was.

"No luck?"

He shook his head. "We'd barely had a chance to pull onto the Boulevard before dispatch called us back."

Shawn searched the crowd, trying to locate the area where the golden figure of a man had stood only moments before.

"Just as I thought."

Darren turned to him. "What did you think?"

"Have you ever seen that street performer before tonight—the one dressed like a statue?"

"Yeah. I saw him over by the hotel that burned that night. He was performing—oh, I don't know—about a block or so from there the incident took place. Why?"

"And that's the only other time you've seen him?"

"I guess. I probably only remember him at all because of what happened that night. I'm sure I must've seen him other places but just didn't pay attention."

"I don't know..."

"What are you getting at Everly?"

"Just some weird coincidences that make me wonder."

"Well, tell the lieutenant. He said they were willing to consider all angles." Darren glanced to his side and pointed. "Oh hey, there he is now."

Shawn spun around. Although he did see Lieutenant Campos, he also saw Trent and Lee behind him. They were keeping vigil by their engine. He inhaled a sharp breath and averted his gaze right as Trent had spotted him. As he made his way to the lieutenant, he chanced a quick peek and was relieved to see that Trent had angled his body away from him.

After all they'd been through emotionally, he'd almost felt slighted, but reminded himself that Trent was doing the right thing—that this is what they all wanted. It was certainly preferable to Trent yelling and freaking out at him.

Lieutenant Campos acknowledged him as soon as he reached his side. "What is it, Everly?"

He filled his boss in on everything he'd observed that night, as well as his interactions with the mystery woman on other occasions.

"I think you might have something. When you get back to the station tonight, I want you to leave a message with one of the detectives assigned to this investigation, set up a time for you both to meet. We'll need to follow-up on the attacker who was arrested at the motel and see if we can find any additional info that might've been gleaned on that woman, who picked her up, etc." He paused, rubbing his chin. "If you're right, I doubt we'll ever see that statue guy again, but maybe some of the other street performers can give us some info on him. Anything you can think of, Everly." His lieutenant clapped him on the back. "Great observations. That's why we need foot patrol. You guys see what a lot of other officers miss."

"Thank you, sir."

In his peripheral vision, he could barely see Trent. They wouldn't be able to talk for a while, probably not until the following day. He needed him. Incredibly, it hit him hard right at that moment. Trent had become like family to him. Not like the family he'd grown up with, but like what one was supposed to be.

He walked back to where his partner waited. Ben and Jamal had the woman who'd almost been one of the Citizen group's victims on the gurney, and were about to transport her. When he reached Vicki, he could tell she'd been affected by the scene more than usual.

"Do you wanna see about taking a break after this?"

She shrugged. "Maybe."

"Hey, Vicki. What's wrong?"

He'd never seen her so melancholy.

"My sister."

"Your sister?"

He couldn't remember Vicki ever mentioning her before.

"What about her?"

"Her baby daddy used to pimp her out to insure he'd get his next fix. Eventually she was hooked too."

"Meth?"

"The scourge of our society."

"Did she get away from him?"

She made a grunting noise, revulsion and sadness competing expressions on her face. "You could say that."

"How?"

"He was tweaking one night and he set her on fire." She regarded him, her emotions reined back in. "At least she doesn't have to fuck strangers to get a scumbag who claimed to love her his drugs anymore." She lowered her head. "I gotta go check on that girl."

"Yeah, sure." He'd said it softly—he didn't know what else to add.

He watched as she walked away. His gaze was drawn to the dumpster where a team of investigators worked processing evidence, taking photos—the coroner standing by to pick up the remains when the detectives were done.

There were still a few hours left on their shift. As draining as the events of the evening had been so far, Shawn was so worked up he doubted he'd be able to sleep much later. There was a heaviness in the pit of his stomach—Vicki's story only adding more weight to it. He remained in position, insuring that no one from the public made it past the yellow tape protecting the crime scene.

He dug in his pocket for his personal phone. After pulling it out, he stared at it for a long time, wondering if he was making a mistake. Trent probably didn't even have his cell on him. It was most likely back in his room. He wouldn't even see it until later. Making sure no one was around, he quickly typed in a message.

I miss you. Happy dreams.

He tapped the message icon then stuffed the phone back in his pocket. Less than a minute later, he felt his phone buzz. It startled him. After pulling it out again, he swiped the screen and saw that he had a new text message. He opened it and smiled, some of the heaviness lightening.

Only if you're in them.

Chapter Ten

There was a sense of peace within him that was quite unusual, untypical. Trent had spent the majority of his years as a rather calm individual. He wasn't prone to hysterical outbursts or seesawing moods. He was sure that was at least partly why his display at the hotel fire had been so shocking to everyone—himself included. Overall, he wasn't what anyone would ever consider effusive in his behavior. He wasn't loud, didn't draw attention to himself. It certainly wasn't because he was shy, or lacking in confidence. He was a solid self-assured man who believed in the simple joys of life.

Love. That was all he wanted, and Shawn represented love to him. He didn't plan to let Shawn know when he came over that night. It was their first time together since he'd almost destroyed everything that had been building between them. It wasn't the right time yet.

He checked on the chicken pot pies he had in the oven. They had about fifteen or twenty minutes to go, then they'd need to sit for about another ten or so. The salad was ready and he had a Riesling wine chilling in the refrigerator. It felt like their first date.

He had to chuckle to himself when he thought of their supposed first date. How he'd practically corralled Shawn in the station parking garage then essentially dragged him to the diner. He'd learned a lot since then. One of the main things being that it was okay to treat someone with care and affection without it making a statement about his strength or masculinity. And that he didn't have to control absolutely everything—that some things would always be out of his control.

The knock at the door made him jump. He took a couple of deep breaths to let go of some of his nervousness. He told himself that things would be wonderful between him and Shawn—especially if their increasingly dirty texts to one another recently were any indicator. His plan was to shower Shawn with so much love that he wouldn't know what hit him—wouldn't even question it.

As soon as he saw Shawn standing in his entryway he was hard, his erection pushing uncomfortably against his denim pants.

"Hey."

Shawn was delectably attired. They were advancing toward fall, but it was still plenty warm outside. He was all in black—tight jeans and T-shirt—a color he'd never seen Shawn in, no doubt because of the unrelenting sun and heat. It was striking on him. His eyes were drawn to the overnight bag he held in his hand. Even though they'd discussed him spending the night, he hadn't wanted to count on it until Shawn was actually there.

Trent opened his arms, hoping Shawn wouldn't reject him. Instead, a joyous grin split his face and he stepped right into Trent's embrace. They stood in the entrance of his home for at least a few minutes, holding tight. As he inhaled the scent of Shawn, he couldn't stop himself, he needed a taste.

He lowered his mouth over Shawn's lips, parting the seam with his probing tongue. It wasn't his intention to be greedy, to take so hungrily, but his need took over. Shawn answered back with his own eager kisses, spurning Trent on. They clutched and grabbed at one another, their exchange heating until Trent was dizzy with it. Shawn moaned, grinding his obvious erection into Trent's crotch. His movements were so urgent that he pushed Trent against the doorframe with a grunt.

Shawn grabbed his hair and pulled him back, breaking their connection. His breaths were short, gasping.

"Baby. Oh, baby, I've missed you so fucking much."

Trent felt as though he were being climbed like a tree. Shawn had hoisted himself up until his legs were wrapped around Trent's waist, his arms encircling his neck, holding on as if he'd never let go. He cupped Shawn's ass to keep him from falling.

"I have you, Shawn, sweetheart. I've missed you too, so very much. I need you. More than you'll ever know."

It frightened him to say it out loud because it was so true.

"I love you."

Trent gasped. Shawn had said it as he'd stared directly into his eyes, not showing any uncertainty or fear.

"I don't expect you to say it back. I just needed you to know."

Trent captured Shawn's mouth again, sweeping inside with his tongue, deeper each time until they couldn't breathe. He retreated, but kissed Shawn's face, his chin, his neck over and over, Shawn writhing against him.

In between loving on Shawn, he whispered to him. "I've known for a while. Love you too. Didn't want to pressure you."

"Fuck, Trent. Always tell me everything. I wanna know."

He nodded before taking Shawn's mouth again. His honeyed flavor was such an aphrodisiac. Every part of him tasted like heaven. And Trent wanted heaven that night.

Realizing they might be giving the neighbors quite a show and that the dinner he'd spent almost three hours making was about to burn, he carried Shawn inside. He could carry him around forever, wished he could keep him in his pocket. He lowered him on the couch, expecting Shawn to let go so he could get his bag and close the door, but he hung on, wrapping his legs even tighter around Trent's waist. He lost his balance and tumbled forward, rolling at the last minute so as not to crush Shawn.

They both laughed happily, peppering one another with more kisses, their movements growing heated once again. Trent groaned.

"Shawn, the door, the pot pies."

Shawn froze. "Pot pies? As in, an actual pot pie that you made?"

"Yeah."

They were still wrapped around one another, stealing little pecks on one another's faces as they talked.

"That's a quandary."

"That so?"

"Yes. Are they chicken pot pies?"

Trent snorted. "They are."

"Hmm. My favorite. And when will these chicken pot pies be done?"

"In a few minutes."

"And they need to be eaten right away?"

"Actually, they have to sit for about ten to fifteen minutes."

"Perfect."

"Why perfect?"

"That's all the time I need. Mouth or hand?"

Trent hissed. "You are such a rascal. Mouth. But I really think I should close the front door and shut the oven off first."

"Okay, you do that and I'll get naked."

"Jesus."

Trent rushed around taking care of everything, his nuts already tightening in anticipation. Once he returned from the kitchen, he was treated to the most glorious sight ever—Shawn's nude body.

"Want you so bad."

"Want you more, baby."

Tearing his clothes from his body as quickly as he could, Trent kept his gaze trained on Shawn's full cock, the flared head slick and red with his desire. It would be in his mouth soon.

Once he was free from the confines of his clothing, he advanced on Shawn. Right as he reached the couch, Shawn moved to stroke his own dick and Trent slapped his hand away.

"Don't touch. I want every drop that's there on my tongue."

"Then give me that."

Shawn fisted his erection and tugged him forward with it. He wrapped his kiss-swollen lips around the tip, pressing his tongue in the slit. Trent lifted one leg and planted his foot on the sofa cushion next to Shawn. As Shawn lowered his mouth on Trent's shaft, taking more of him in, Trent placed his hand on the back of Shawn's head. He was careful not to push on him, only to cradle him.

His ball sac hung low and heavy, swaying as Shawn sucked him. Shawn had been running his hands up and down Trent's legs as he deep-throated him, but he raised one of them to palm Trent's nuts, manipulating them as he continued to hungrily eat his leaking dick. Shawn increased his suction, flicking his tongue like mad over his glans every time he reached the tip.

"Oh, God, close…"

A surge of energy rushed to his core, his balls tightening. He shot, grabbing onto Shawn's shoulder with one hand as he pitched forward. He stopped himself with his other hand, falling against the back of the couch as the force of his orgasm carried him onward. A strangled sound was wrenched from his mouth as Shawn continued to draw his climax out, milking him with his lips, his tongue.

Out of breath from Shawn's amazing blow job, his knees buckled. He finally rolled all the way onto the couch, Shawn allowing Trent's sated flesh to fall from his mouth. He covered his eyes with one arm, the rest of him melted and splayed on the sofa.

"Unreal. I don't think I can move."

Shawn crawled up next to him and cuddled to his side. Trent raised the arm he'd had over his face and wrapped it around Shawn, pulling him closer. He nuzzled his head before whispering to him.

"Now you."

"I can wait." Shawn chuckled, obviously satisfied with himself. "You seem a tad spent."

"You can face fuck, can't you? Use me."

The change in Shawn's body language was instantaneous. Shawn tensed then quickly straddled him. It was clear that Trent's idea had been met with approval. Trent cupped Shawn's ass again, encouraging him higher.

"Come on, give me that hard cock. Paint my lips with your cum."

"Fuck, Trent, your voice. Let me at least get it in your mouth before I nut all over."

A low rumble of laughter came up from Trent's chest. "Here, lay it on my tongue."

He relaxed his head against the cushion and opened his mouth wide, sticking out the promised tongue. Shawn appeared dazed, heady with lust. He rose up on the couch until he stood, angling the soft steel of his shaft until the tip lay where Trent had requested. Shawn let loose a groaning sigh, clutching Trent's hair and shoulder to keep his balance.

Trent wrapped his lips around the mushroomed head, suckling only the end, pulling him in, urging him on.

"Uhnh, oh shit, Trent, baby."

Shawn placed both hands on the couch on either side of Trent and moved in and out of his mouth in short, rapid thrusts. Trent traced his fingers along the backs of Shawn's thighs, playing in the hair, softly caressing his ass. He ghosted two digits over his hole, already anticipating what he wanted to do to Shawn later that night. He slid his hand down his taint then teased the underside of his sac gently, sweetly.

The instant Shawn's balls drew up, he grabbed him at the root and pulled off his cock.

"Trent, I'm gonna…"

As soon as he had Shawn's dick free of his mouth, he pointed it at his face.

"*Yeah*, come now."

Shawn spurted his release in short, milky jets as Trent used Shawn's cock to rub the cum on his lips, all over his cheeks. Twitching and jerking, Shawn continued to pump into Trent's fist, Trent squeezing more seed from him. Shawn fumbled between them, loosening Trent's grip on his member. Once he was free, he dropped down on his knees to take Trent's mouth, licking up his own juices then sharing it with Trent on a kiss.

He was deliciously and thoroughly satisfied. They kneaded and caressed one another some more, the smell and stickiness of their encounter marked all over them.

Trent captured Shawn's bottom lip between his teeth and gently pulled.

"Those pies should be ready by now." He felt gloriously wicked. "Even though we already ate."

Shawn raised his eyebrows. "Listen to you. Well, I considered that an appetizer."

"And the main course?"

"That's after the pies."

* * * *

Nude again, Shawn was sprawled on his stomach across Trent's bed, a pillow tucked under his chin, his arms wrapped around it. Trent was downstairs locking up the house and getting them more wine. He'd instructed Shawn to be naked and ready for him when he returned.

After their earlier encounter, they'd only put their underwear back on, so naked hadn't been that far of a trip. They'd shared an amazing meal—he could seriously become accustomed to Trent's culinary expertise—and had curled up on the couch afterwards, touching and talking. The truly remarkable part of the evening was how willing Trent had been to tell stories of his life, to really converse. Other than the sessions with Dr Silver, he'd never heard Trent form so many sentences together all at once. He still wouldn't categorize him as a chatterbox—nor did he want him to be—but he sensed it came from a place of trust that Trent was so willing to open up with him.

His chest constricted a little at the thought of almost losing Trent. He shouldn't be thinking of such things, but it was highlighted by their earlier confessions of love. He'd honestly been surprised. Going by what he'd already experienced with Trent, knowing his manner, he'd thought Trent might be one of those guys that could never actually say the words—that Shawn might have had to follow little bread crumbs through a dark forest to get to the truth.

"Are you ready for me to take care of that sweet ass?"

It hadn't been the greeting he'd expected, but he decided Trent's was much better than any other he could've hoped for.

"I can't imagine ever saying no to that."

"Good. I'm going to jump in the shower and rinse off. I'll be right back."

Shawn leaped off the bed. "Hey, wait for me."

Trent offered his hand and they laced their fingers together.

"This'll be quick. I'm anxious to play with your hot little hole."

"Fuck, Trent."

He grasped his dick without thinking. The filthy words uttered in the low growl of Trent's voice were the only real turn on he would ever need.

True to his word, they were in there for only a few minutes. It could've easily gone longer, but Trent kept pulling Shawn's hands away from both of their shafts, finally smacking his butt to get him to stop. Once they stepped out of the stall, Trent toweled him off—and as expected—scooped him up and carried him to the bed. He laid him down, then stepped back, eyeing him greedily.

"Love you."

Shawn grinned, his heart full again. "Love you too."

"I want tonight to be better than you've ever had."

"Trent, you're already better than I've ever had."

"I want you to have more, more than you even knew you wanted. And I'll be the only one who'll ever give it to you."

He couldn't breathe deeply enough, Trent's words had surrounded him, filled him.

"Trust me."

Shawn nodded, his cock straining, throbbing with need. "I will. I do."

"Then get on all fours, facing the headboard."

"Fuck." He'd muttered it as he'd positioned himself. Trent had been an immediate attraction for him, a sexual beacon that he'd flocked to. But since they'd been together, he'd seemed to transform into more and more of a lusty horn dog.

"Nice, very nice. I'm going to loosen you up real nice. Make you beg."

Begging already.

The way he was displayed gave him a sense of incredible vulnerability. He heard a drawer open behind him and began to twist around to peer over his shoulder.

"No looking."

He snapped his head forward. The mattress dipped behind him and he knew that Trent was right there, Trent's face level with his open ass cheeks. He jerked, almost losing his balance when Trent's warm breath fanned across his exposed crease. Trent lightly tapped his opening, teasing it, making tiny circles around it.

"Your hole responds to my every little touch. Mmm."

Shawn exhaled on a loud moan as Trent's tongue slid up his crack, slow and wet. He laved his backside completely, dipping below to suckle the loose skin of his sac, taking small nips of his sensitive flesh around his entrance, and flicking his pucker with the hardened tip of his tongue.

Trent's attentions increased in their fervor, each lick, each exploration more insistent than the last. Finally, Trent seemed to focus all his energy on Shawn's eager hole, pushing, prodding until Trent had forced his tongue past Shawn's tight rim. He fucked him with it, Shawn feeling how Trent's entire face was buried in his ass, noises akin to growls pouring out of Trent.

When he retreated, the loss of Trent's mouth on him was palpable. Shawn couldn't help a small whimper that fell from his lips. He felt the soothing caress of Trent's large hand on his lower back.

"Shh, there's much more. Drop to your elbows, it'll be easier and make it better too."

He was dying to know what 'it' was. They'd never fucked in the position he was in, so he thought that might be what Trent had planned. The sensation of the lube in his crease seemed to confirm his thoughts and he was anxious to be filled with Trent's large shaft.

Trent breached him almost immediately with two fingers, stretching him nicely. He pushed back against the intrusion, hungry for more—much more. He pulled out and Shawn prepared himself to be penetrated by Trent's rigid flesh. Instead, there was an unyielding object pressed to his anus.

My dildo.

His small gasp must have been telling.

"You left something here. I've been aching to use this on you, to make you come with it stuffed up your ass."

"Trent..."

He wanted to tell him to quit talking or the toy would never make it past his rim before he shot all over the bed covers. But his breath was stolen when the tip of the dildo opened him up by a fraction. There couldn't be more than half an inch of the object inside him, but it was enough to make him fall on his heels.

"Okay, yes, I'm begging. Please put it in."

"I will. Eventually.

Trent slid his hand under his stomach and encouraged him to stick his rear back in the air.

"That's it. Let's try that again, stay still and let me control it."

It was even worse than before. Trent slid it around the outer ring of his hole, almost poking it in a few times, only to go back to circling it again. Shawn clutched at his hair, the top of his head pressed to the pillow, his asshole aching for more attention.

He felt more lube on his crack, but it had been warmed—the way Trent had promised from before. The unyielding object pressed against his opening again and with a pop, breached him by what couldn't be more than an inch. Trent continued to poke it in, take it completely out then stab it in with a short thrust.

Trent repeated the same motions in rapid succession until Shawn's entire world consisted of nothing other than his sensitized rim. Cries—keening, sounds Shawn knew he'd never made before—Trent's actions forced them from his body as Shawn endured the erotic torture. The noises turned into pleas, and Trent was right. He was begging. He did it without shame from a place of nothing but pure need.

He cried out when the toy sank all the way into his passage until he felt Trent's hand resting against his butt cheeks. There was no movement and he grunted, using his elbows to push against it, to encourage Trent to do something with it. Anything.

"Up on all fours again."

"Trent, I'm seriously pleading with you here. Do *not* take that fucking thing out of me, I'm right at the edge."

"Don't you dare come yet."

Trent grabbed the base of Shawn's cock and squeezed. Hard.

Shawn had made it on all fours again, but when Trent had gripped him so tight, he almost fell back down. Maintaining his hold on Shawn's dick, Trent maneuvered beneath him until he'd lined his mouth up with Shawn's swollen erection. Wrapping one arm around Shawn's waist, he yanked him down, swallowing around him, using his other hand to manipulate the dildo in him.

He rutted in Trent's mouth, driven on by the toy he was being fucked with and Trent's enthusiastic sucking. He was a ball of sensation driven by unbelievable need. His hardened length was wrapped by Trent's soft lips and suckled by his hot tongue. Then he would push down Trent's throat, the muscles squeezing his tip so good. His hole was slippery and stretched, each plunge of the dildo pegging his gland.

He couldn't wait any more.

A loud yell sounded, wrenched from him as he came down Trent's throat repeatedly, jerking, clamping his inner muscles around the unyielding object buried deep in his ass. Trent had stilled, holding it there as he continued to suck him dry. His muscles shook, burned. His heart hammered in his chest as he fought a wave of dizziness.

The toy was oh so slowly removed, his passage closing around the large dildo as it exited his body. He could still barely breathe and didn't have the energy to even move one bit. Trent still lay under him, finally releasing his flaccid member, letting it fall from his lips. He nuzzled Shawn's crotch, rubbing his nose in his pubic hair.

After a few minutes, Trent eased out from under him. He kissed the side of his neck and whispered in his ear.

"Stay right there, on your elbows, your ass open for me."

He was spent, really sated. But what Trent had said made his dick twitch with interest. It was unlikely he'd get it up again for round three, but there was still some life there.

The sound of the condom wrapper tearing alerted him that what he'd thought was originally going to happen was about to occur. Trent would fill him from behind with his long, thick cock. He was loose and ready to feel Trent inside him.

Trent's first thrust was slow and deep, taking Trent all the way to the end of his insides. He didn't want to come again—he only wanted to experience Trent's pleasure as he took it from Shawn's body. To know that when his lover came, it was because they'd been joined together.

Trent moved, leisurely at first, then with more power. He angled himself differently with each plunge, seemingly lost in his own sensation. His pace quickened as he slammed more forcefully into Shawn, their skin slapping together. Shawn's half-hard cock bobbed and as Trent's moans increased, his fingers digging deeper in the flesh around Shawn's hips, Shawn squeezed his passage around Trent's dick. That was what did it.

Trent covered him like a cocoon, wrapping an arm around his stomach and pulling him flush to his body as he emptied his seed into the condom. He nipped at the skin on Shawn's upper back, making unintelligible sounds as he rode out his climax. He stayed like that for several minutes, holding Shawn, resting his face on Shawn's shoulder, placing light kisses here and there.

Finally, he rolled to his side, bringing Shawn with him. As soon as he'd done that, his softened dick slid from Shawn's ass, and he reached between them to grab the condom. They lay silent for a while, Shawn resting in Trent's arms, his back to Trent's chest. To be lying together, skin to skin, peaceful in the afterglow of their lovemaking—was all that Shawn wanted. There was so much waiting for them, so much more to look forward to. Their life together was only beginning.

Chapter Eleven

The previous two weeks had bordered on perfect. The only thing that had prevented absolute perfection were the days he and Trent couldn't be together because of their job responsibilities. They'd fallen into a routine where Shawn would stay at Trent's home when he had to be at the firehouse so that he could see him the moment he came back. Of course, once he was there, Trent didn't want him to leave. Other than a couple of nights they'd spent at Shawn's place, he'd practically moved in at Trent's.

Shawn sat in the break room at work, grinning to himself. He took a sip of his coffee, hoping that anyone who might spot him in there wouldn't think he'd turned into a complete lunatic. His smile couldn't be helped. When he got off his shift that night, he'd be on his way to Trent's where he'd been told a new toy had arrived in the mail. Trent refused to tell him what it was, so of course, it was all he could think about. They would have the next couple of days to play with whatever it was.

"You're disgusting."

He choked on his coffee, almost dropping it at the sound of Vicki's voice. He had a brief moment of panic where he wondered if he'd spoken his thoughts out loud.

"What do you mean?"

She pulled out a chair and sat down, stretching her legs out, crossing her arms in front of her.

"Hmmph. You're like the cat that ate the canary every day around here. It's disgusting." She looked around to see if anyone was close enough to hear them. "Aren't you glad you took my advice, Everly?"

"Very. Things are better than I ever could have imagined."

She arched her eyebrows. "I'm glad. But please, no blow-by-blow descriptions."

He'd just taken another sip and choked again.

"Dammit, Vicki. Are you trying to kill me?"

She snorted. "What sort of plans do you and lover boy have scheduled for your days off? You'd better take advantage, since they don't always fall at the same time."

"Yeah, no kidding. Not sure." He cleared his throat. "I'm headed over there tonight after work. He's been back from the station since noon, so I know he'll have cooked up something special."

"You are one lucky son of a bitch."

He smiled. "I know. He's a wonderful man."

"I meant the cooking. I don't care about the rest of it."

He pursed his lips at her.

Darren stuck his head in the room. "Hey, everyone. The lieutenant has some sort of important announcement."

People rose to their feet with a scrape of chairs and some disgruntled mumblings to head to the briefing room.

Vicki regarded him. "Citizens Group?"

He sighed in resignation. "Most likely."

The information he'd given the detectives had been enough to work with that they'd been able to at least track down the man who'd been arrested. Upon questioning him, they'd uncovered ties that he had with a few extreme religious cults. None of them were locally based however, so they'd had to team with the FBI to speak with the out-of-state groups. LVMPD still believed he was involved somehow, but they hadn't been able to locate the woman he'd been accused of attacking and who'd told Shawn about the man in the trailer.

The other interesting bit of info had been when the detectives had questioned the man Shawn had saved. He claimed he never took sleeping pills but did accept coffee from a woman who'd been by the trailer a few times to chat with him. Based on that, the detectives were certain that Shawn had been justified in his suspicions about the mystery woman.

When they entered the room, he noted that it was even more crowded than usual. He saw some of his fellow foot patrol officers who worked other shifts. They were there in their street clothes, so they must've been called in specifically for the meeting. Lieutenant Campos strolled in and made his way to the front of the room. He was trailed by two of the lead investigators on the team that had been formed to deal with the Citizen's Against Immorality Group.

The lieutenant began, "I'm going to speak briefly before turning everything over to our investigators. I don't think I need to elaborate on that. We all know why they're here. I want to reiterate that this is a very sensitive situation, but we need to all be on our toes. Thanks to Officer Everly's astute observations, we were able to locate one viable suspect who we hope can lead us to others involved with this heinous group of people."

He turned to the other two men, nodding. "Gentlemen."

One of them stepped forward. "I think most of you know me here as Detective Isaacson. Along with my partner, Detective Lewis, we're heading the team that is handling this investigation. There have been some recent developments in the case that we aren't at liberty to disclose at this time, but we do need your help with something. We're about to hand out a composite picture of the mystery woman we've been trying to locate. Now, I'm sure most of you have seen it already, but please take another look, keep it with you while you're out there. It's vital that we pick her up as soon as possible.

"The other thing I'd like to bring up—and the reason why we called you all in here today—is that we believe someone is leaking information to the press. There's been more than one story that has cited anonymous sources from the police department. That wouldn't be such an issue except that certain facts that no one would have known any other way were published. Let's be perfectly clear so that there's no question. Anyone caught giving classified information...really, *any* information to the media will be terminated immediately, with possible charges, depending on the nature of the information."

Both he and Vicki exchanged glances. Who would be dumb enough to do such a thing? After a few more general announcements from the lieutenant, they readied themselves to head out on the street to face another night. Once they were outside, on their beat, the gloom of the briefing lifted somewhat. The evening was pleasantly warm, not hot. The impending fall had taken the sharp edge off the heat.

He strolled along with Vicki at his side, the possibility of locating the mystery woman never leaving the forefront of his mind. He didn't need a composite drawing. He'd never forget her face. There had been no new killing, no new arson attempts recently. While it was a good thing, it also kept everyone on high alert as if waiting for the other shoe to drop.

His mind wandered again to Trent, as it often did. Since Trent was at home, undoubtedly planning some sort of wicked interlude to go along with whatever had arrived in the mail, Shawn wouldn't have to go to extra lengths if emergency services were called out. There hadn't been any more problems since Trent had returned to work, and he meant to keep it that way. Even though Trent had told him that he would've left Vegas if things hadn't worked out between them, left his job, he didn't want that for his lover. He wanted Trent to get everything—his career and love. He wanted the same thing for himself.

Tires screeched and cars swerved as a young woman ran into the Boulevard traffic. One car wasn't able to stop in time and slammed into her. Screams rang out, several people rushing to her aid, the rest of the crowds gathering to watch. He sprinted behind Vicki to help her control the chaos and tend to the victim. Something about the whole scenario nagged at him. It was too reminiscent of the hotel fire, the motel attacker.

He stopped where he was, his gaze traveling around the area, alert to anything that might seem out of place. There wasn't anything he could pinpoint, but his gut still told him that something was off. He picked up his pace again, anxious to get to where the crowds had all been drawn, to back up Vicki.

As he passed a large hedge outside one of the casinos, the mystery woman stepped out in front of him. He froze, too stunned to speak. She glared at him, hatred shining in her eyes. He mentally shook himself then lunged for her. Someone grabbed and yanked him back. The defensive training he'd learned kicked in, but before he could do anything, the woman yelled out.

"We have your lover!"

He frowned. What the hell was she talking about? It was ridiculous. He'd spoken to Trent…

Over three hours ago.

His gut clenched, his heart rate accelerating as he fought down the fear over his lover's safety.

"I don't know what you're talking about."

"I think you do, Officer Everly."

He spun around to face the man who'd grabbed his arm initially. It was one of the goons who'd razzed him about Trent when they first got together—the one from the break room. For the life of him, he couldn't remember the guy's name, and he was dressed in street clothes.

"What's all this about?"

He couldn't reconcile what the mystery woman and a fellow officer were doing together.

"It's about sick deviants like you and your so-called boyfriend, Trent Marshall. I told my mother all about you two. How you're flaunting your perversion to everyone, the police force, the fire stations."

"You're absolutely insane. I don't believe for a moment you have Trent." He racked his brain for something to catch them in their lie. "Especially since he's at the station right now. "

The woman spoke up. "That would be difficult, since we sent some of our people to his house to get him earlier. I was told he was in the middle of preparing a lovely meal. It's so sad that you won't be able to enjoy it with him." Her hate-filled stare returned. "Or any of the other sick things both of you freaks do."

He clenched his teeth. It wouldn't do Trent any good if he fell apart. He tried to surreptitiously gauge if anyone had noticed them or if any of his fellow officers were nearby.

"Quit stalling. Come with us unless you want your lover to die alone."

The woman's son, one of his supposed work associates, relieved him of his weapon then latched onto his arm, tugging him past the large hedge and toward a walkway between the casino and parking garage. He still wasn't completely convinced that they actually had Trent, but he couldn't take the chance. And if they didn't have him, maybe it would be an opportunity to bring the group down. Although, since one of the men who worked for the police was closely involved, things didn't look so good for him—Shawn would not be a witness they would want to keep around.

They led him to a service elevator in the back of the garage where the son shoved him inside. They both boarded after him then pressed the button to the fourth floor. Shawn noted that there were only five stories to the garage. He had absolutely no idea where they were going—or why.

As soon as the doors slid open, the son shoved him out by the barrel of the gun. Everything was very dim in the gray cement wall interior. The son never let him go, maintaining a tight grip on his arm. Truthfully, he could have easily fought him off, but for the fact that the other guy had his Glock. He also needed to find out if they really had Trent first before he made any moves.

A plain, unmarked door stood at the end of the hall. It reminded Shawn of what would shield a typical commercial utility closet. The woman tapped out a distinctive knock and Shawn fought off the urge to chuckle at the silly school yard style behavior. The door flung open then he was roughly escorted inside. To his horror, Trent was indeed in there. Two men flanked his lover, each one pointing a gun at him. His insides liquefied. They locked eyes and Shawn tried not to upset Trent by showing any fear. But the fear was there—it was evident in Trent's wide-eyed expression.

"I think it's time we perform the cleansing ritual."

Cleansing ritual?

He was certain that whoever this woman was, she had somehow appointed herself humanity's judge and was filled with an unhealthy dose of her own self-importance. And she watched too much bad television. Unfortunately for him and Trent, it didn't make her or her armed cohorts any less dangerous.

The armed men forcefully corralled them, but carefully kept apart from one another. Every time the woman looked at either him or Trent, she had an ugly sneer on her face. He'd also noted that other than when the son had grabbed his arm out on the sidewalk, all the men were careful to only touch him and Trent with the barrels of their guns as if they were diseased or something.

Shawn tried to catch Trent's attention, desperate to wordlessly convey to him his love. It was even possible they could somehow signal to one another as well. Trent was a big guy and Shawn knew he was strong too. Surely between the two of them they could take out the psychos holding them?

The son smacked him across the face.

"Quit trying to look at him!"

Trent lunged for the man who'd hit him, but the son immediately pointed his gun to Shawn's temple.

"I wouldn't."

Trent halted, his eyes filled with such an agony that Shawn wasn't sure he could bear it. They proceeded to a set of steps at the far end then climbed the stairs to one small landing before taking the next set that alternated in the other direction. They reached the roof of the garage. His breath hitched and a cold sweat broke out on his skin as soon as he saw it.

A pile of oily rags and two cans of gasoline sat in the center of the parking structure. Two coiled ropes lay nearby.

Oh no. Fuck no.

"Like the whores of Babylon who we cleansed before you, your filthy souls will be released upon your death."

A rapid succession of shots rang out and before he'd barely had a chance to register what was happening, the three armed men lay on the ground, dead from gunshot wounds. SWAT team members burst from the shadows and from behind cars, shouting for the woman to surrender.

An agonized howl escaped her as she dove for the rags and gasoline, throwing herself on them. If they fired at her, they could all go up in flames.

"Everyone back!"

Trent lunged for him, gathering him up and running as fast as he could until they were on the other side of the cement barrier. A *whoosh* sounded, followed by a ball of fire and the shrill screams of the woman as she burned. He couldn't look. It was too gruesome. So senseless.

His lover lowered him until his feet touched the ground, but didn't let him go, cradling him to his chest.

"Shawn, oh my God, I was so terrified for you."

"I was scared for you too, baby. I'm so relieved you're okay."

Trent let go to cup his face.

"You're not mad at me?"

Shawn looked at him in confusion. "Why would I be mad?"

"I carried you in front of everybody."

It hadn't even occurred to him. "You protected me. How could I be mad about that?"

There was a glimmer of tears in Trent's eyes. "Then I hope you don't get mad about this either."

Trent claimed his mouth with a deep kiss—one that left no doubt to anyone watching what they were to one another. Shawn wasn't the slightest bit mad.

* * * *

Their cabin at the Tecopa Hot Springs Resort was nice but quaint. Shawn didn't really give a shit one way or the other. All he cared about was that he and Trent had the whole week off together to soak in the mineral baths, go on hikes, do some camping—and fuck each other like bunnies. He snickered.

It had been over a month since their all-too-real brush with death. If it hadn't been for Trent's quick thinking, things might have turned out much grimmer. Ever since their high school days together, Trent and Lee had their own little codes. As they'd gotten older and had begun to work in emergency services, they'd utilized some of their youthful tactics. They had a mutual agreement that if one or the other of them were to call and leave the line open without saying anything, it meant they needed help. It had only failed once before when Lee had to learn the hard way not to butt dial anyone when he'd had an older model phone. His girlfriend had been terrified when the police showed up at his place.

But it had been instrumental in saving their lives. When the mystery woman, who they'd since discovered had the simple moniker of Ann Spencer, had sent her minions to Trent's place, he'd managed to give the emergency signal. Lee had contacted the police, who'd immediately put a tail on Shawn. The combination of what Shawn had told them about the woman, the internal leak of information within the department and his relationship to Trent meant they were sure he'd be a target too. With Trent leaving his phone in his pocket, it had allowed them to pinpoint his position and bring in the SWAT team. When they'd spotted the rags and gasoline, they'd huddled into position, waiting until the armed perpetrators were out in the open.

The entire experience had been much too close of a call for them both, and Trent had needed to see Dr Silver for some additional sessions on his own. They'd finally been able to arrange some time away, which the therapist had also suggested.

Shawn had already unpacked their things. He was reclining on the queen-sized bed, waiting for Trent to return from the front desk. He was making reservations for them to enjoy one of the private hot mineral baths.

The door unlocked and the man he loved with all his heart ambled in. He still wondered what he'd done to deserve such a fine male specimen. More importantly, to deserve someone who was so loving and giving.

He propped himself up on his elbows. "What's the bath report?"

Trent sat next to him on the bed, eyeing him, running his hand along Shawn's torso.

"Not for two hours."

Trent's soothing caresses had already amped him up into a high state of arousal. He let out a groan.

"What do you suggest we do with our time?"

Trent leaned over him to take a kiss, pressing his hand against Shawn's belly as he did. He slid his hand lower, placing more pressure on his lower abdomen. Shawn moaned into the sensation. Trent released his mouth, but continued to manipulate him right above his pubis. His cock was so hard that it was uncomfortably jammed against the zipper of his jeans.

"You did really well on the drive up here."

Shawn's head lolled back as Trent continued the motion of his hand.

"Speak for yourself. Those winding curves were evil."

Trent's low, rumbling laugh seemed to shoot right up his spine. The man's voice was hard-wired to his dick.

"Pegged you nicely, didn't it? That's why I wanted you to wear it for the drive."

"I almost came in my pants several times."

"But you were good, so that means you get a nice fucking before the hot baths."

"Please tell me that fucking is happening soon."

Trent chuckled and stood up. Shawn exhaled when his lover removed his hand, not sure if he was relieved or sorry. The external stimulation of his prostate was something they'd learned together once they'd become interested in getting more toys to add to Shawn's dildo. Never had he been so glad to be caught in his whole life. It had opened up a whole new world of sexual exploration for them both.

Trent removed his grooming kit from the top drawer of the small dresser. He got the necessary items ready then undressed slowly, his gaze never leaving Shawn as he did.

"Faster. Please?"

"God, I love how you beg."

Once Trent was completely nude, he undressed Shawn. It had become one of Trent's things—he always wanted to be the one to take Shawn's clothes off.

He patted his hip as soon as Shawn was naked.

"On your stomach."

Sometimes he liked to top Trent or to guide their love play, but what he really enjoyed was how Trent took charge of him in the bedroom.

"Now tuck your knees up under your body."

After he'd followed Trent's orders, he was brazenly exposed to his lover's gaze. His ass was available for whatever Trent desired. He tapped a finger on the end of the plug, the small vibrations sending sparks through him every time his gland was hit. Trent grasped the base of the toy and twisted slowly, eliciting more groans from him.

"Anything Trent—I'll do anything if you'll replace that thing in me with your cock."

"Mmm. That's quite an offer. How about you have to wear the plug the next time we have the guys over from the station?"

"Are you mental?"

"Mental over you."

"I don't know…"

Trent released the plug and shifted away, as if he were going to stand.

"If you're not sure, we can wait until later…"

"Fuck! No, I surrender. Cock now, plug later."

Trent eased back onto the bed. He placed his hand on Shawn's lower back and stroked his skin in a slow circle. He lowered his head so his lips were right next to Shawn's ear.

"I am so in love with you."

Shawn sighed. "Love you too, baby."

Trent used his warm, wet tongue to explore the inside of Shawn's ear. He continued to kiss and touch him, finally reaching down to twist the plug, urging it loose. He tugged on it, Shawn's body not quick to relinquish its hold on the bulbous object. Shawn pushed out to help with its removal, the widest part still a wonder as it massively stretched him.

Once it was free, the hollow ache in him needed to be filled right away. Trent was sheathed, ready to give him what he needed. Surrounding Shawn with his large body and cocooning him like he'd done before, Trent easily slid home, burying himself in Shawn's slick ass. It didn't take either one of them long to cry out their release, the build-up on the trip there all the foreplay they'd needed.

Afterwards, they lay in one another's embraces, their limbs tangled together, their soft dicks nestled against each other.

He could hear Trent reflexively swallowing from where he had his ear pressed against his chest.

"Out with it. What's on your mind?"

"When we get back, back home, I don't want to take you back to your place."

"Oh. Sure. I can stay at your house until I have to go back to work."

"That's not what I meant."

Shawn lifted his head to meet Trent's gaze.

"Okay. What did you mean?"

Trent stroked his head, stared at him intently the way he'd been doing from almost the first moment they'd met.

"I mean come live with me. All the time. Move in."

It all came crashing in on him. Trent was his. He was Trent's. Of course they should live together.

"Okay."

A large smile spread across Trent's face, one that was rarely seen, but all the more precious because of it.

"Okay."

The baths were forgotten as they celebrated the beginning of their new life. Together.

About the Author

Erotic Romance author Morticia Knight enjoys a good saucy tale, with MM and MMF pairings. Since she loves several genres, you may find your heroes in a contemporary, historical, paranormal or sci-fi setting. One of her passions is bringing people's fantasies to life on the page, because life is too short for even one boring moment. Her stories are volcanic in heat, deep in emotion, and sprinkled with doses of humor.

When not indulging in her passion for books, she loves the outdoors, film and music. The Pacific Northwest is the ideal spot to enjoy both hiking and beachcombing. Once upon a time she was the singer in an indie rock band that toured the West Coast and charted on U.S. college radio. She currently resides on the northern coast of Oregon, where the constant rain and fog remind her of visits to her family in England and Scotland when she was a child.

She is currently working on a new historical MM series, as well as a steampunk horror and sci-fi ménage.

Morticia Knight loves to hear from readers. You can find her contact information, website details and author profile page at http://www.totallybound.com.

Totally Bound Publishing

TOTALLY BOUND

Home of Erotic Romance

CPSIA information can be obtained
at www.ICGtesting.com
Printed in the USA
FSOW01n0913081014
3212FS

9 781784 302405